# RUNNING TOGETHER

## EINAV AFLALO

Einav Aflalo
Running Together

Publihsed by BooxAi

ISBN: 978-965-577-904-2

# CHAPTER 1

ANNA HEARD A BELL RINGING BEHIND HER. EARLIER, SHE WAS told to get down on all fours and after she did, she stayed like that for a while. Now, her knees started to ache. Nevertheless, she was so terrified she didn't have the guts to get up, or even move an inch. The door opened and HE walked in. Looking at the ground, she could only see his shoes; but she was certain it was HIM.

'I have a gift for you, my beloved pet,' he said, almost happily. She raised her head, looking up at him and heard the ringing sound again. He was holding up a pink strip with a bell in the middle; the kind cats wear for collars.

'Come here, Kitty,' he called her, the same way people usually call their cats. She was so shaken; she couldn't move. 'Kitty,' he said, in a more aggressive tone, 'come here.'

Her body moved against her will. She dragged her knees on the floor and sat beneath him. 'Good Kitty,' he praised her. He was different from Sara, she thought. Sara used to praise her as well, back when this whole thing started. But, somehow, when he said those words, it didn't make her happy like Sara did. On the contrary, it made her want to throw up.

He put the bell collar around her neck, tied it and said. 'Cats don't wear clothes, Kitty,' he was referring to her school uniforms. 'Take them off,' he said in that aggressive tone again. Anna sat on the floor and started taking off her clothes while this man watched her. Now, she wore nothing but the bell collar he gave her.

He allowed her to get up now. She stood in front of him on her two feet; and somehow, this felt more painful than sitting on her knees. She fought the urge to cover herself; knowing that, if she'll do that, he will get mad again. Her left eye was still purple-bluish from the last time he did.

He opened his pants, took them and his underwear off and sat on the chair. He marked her with his finger to come closer to him. Once she did, he pulled her up and sat her on his lap. He looked at her, waiting. Anna closed her eyes when she had to put him inside her. Her tears fell on their own as she moved against his body, hating every second of it.

He didn't say much after he was done with her. He got his way, and that was that. He threw her on the ground and got up to put his clothes back on. The door closed behind him while she was lying on the floor, crying. She knew she had to stay there, alone in that room, until the next time he'll show up.

# CHAPTER 2

ANNA WOKE UP SCREAMING; SHE SAT UP AND TRIED TO CATCH her breath. Lightning flashed on her face followed by a strong sound of thunder. Her cheeks were itching from the tears she was crying during her sleep and her pajama was full of sweat. Again. Five years have passed since that happened, but in her dreams, it felt like it was still happening right now.

Anna looked quickly to her side. Her roommate, Lily, was still asleep. Few! Thank god! Lily was wearing her ear plugs and was sleeping like a baby, a nineteen-year-old baby, but still... Anna was scared she had woken her up again; since she has been waking Lily almost every night over the last year or so. That is, until Lily got her ear plugs.

Anna took her phone and looked at the time. Eight-thirty in the morning. 'Shit!' she jumped off the bed. 'I'm late.' She thought, grabbed some clothes off the floor, wore them, combed her hair, wiped her face with some tissues and looked at the reflection on the phone. 'Good enough,' she said and rushed to the bathrooms at the other end of the floor, barefoot.

Her and Lily's room was on the end of the second floor of the on-campus dorms. They moved there after the many complaints they had gotten, last year, over her midnight screams. She was thankful for the quiet this room provided, with its distance from the world; but it also made everything, including getting ready for class, much more difficult. She wasn't the type who was late on the regular, but after she started living here, it was investable.

After brushing her teeth, wiping her face again and blowing her nose, she rushed back to the room. She immediately threw her things at the bed, put on some deodorant, a jacket and her shoes on. Then she threw a few notebooks, pens and books into her bag and rushed out. Her bag giggles on her back as she rushes through the rain to the computer-science building.

The class starts at nine; and luckily for Anna, she somehow managed to get there on time. The professor walked in the second she sat down and immediately started to teach. Anna was drenched from the rain and wet everything around her, including her desk, chair, and some of the class' floor. Her bag was also drenched with water, but she somehow managed to find a semi-dried notebook in it, and she started taking notes.

When it comes to school work or studying, Anna was, and still is, the best. Especially when it comes to computers. It's like something inside her brain changes; when someone starts talking about it or shows her something that's related to technology. Her eyes light up, and like a crazy scientist, she invents.

People might say she's lucky. She missed a year back in high school and still managed to get accepted to college; and she got a full scholarship to the computer science department, no less. But Anna's mind works in a certain way that it is impossible for her not to be this way. And the last five years contributed much in that aspect. Even though she changed schools after that, Anna preferred numbers and equations over getting to know the other girls; at least the questions in her books she could answer...

Not having friends can be lonely only if one puts their mind into it. But Anna filled her time with classes, books and homework to the level of not having the time to think about anything else. She even took a few curses from the business-management department during her summer vacation, to fill up the spare time. She has devoted herself completely to a life of reading, writing, programming, and calculating. After all, math can never hurt you.

The class was about to end when the professor mentioned a book, about the subject they have been studying, that they could borrow from the library if they want to elaborate on the subject. Anna's eyes lid up. The second the professor announced the class was over, she rushed outside and ran to the library. The stupid rain was still pouring and it seemed it had gotten stronger now.

When she got there, the librarian, Martha, an old but vibrant woman, told her someone had already checked out that book. 'Don't you have another copy, maybe?' Anna asked, panting and moving her wet hair behind her shoulder. 'I'm sorry, dear, we don't,' Martha answered, knowing she's disappointing the poor kid. 'But I think they have it in the store on,' she remembered, 'Wait here, I'll go get a pen and give you the address.' She turned back and went inside her office.

Anna sighed. 'Thank God,' she smiled. She managed to catch her breath by the time Martha finally got back. She gave Anna a semi-torn piece of paper and said, 'I hope you can find it there, dear.'

Anna said her 'Thank you' and shaved the piece of paper into her jeans' front pocket before she rushed back to the computer science building; her next class was about to begin.

# CHAPTER 3

THE RAIN WAS POURING HEAVILY ALL DAY LONG. EVEN WHEN Anna's classes were over and the time was already after six p.m., it kept going. Anna got inside her car and took the piece of paper out of her pocket. It was wet and the ink smeared a bit, but it was still readable. She put the address on the GPS on her phone and started driving.

She had trouble seeing anything through the windshield; too much rain and too much fumes on it made it impossible to keep on going. Anna thought about going back to the dorms and maybe trying again tomorrow, but then something caught her eye at the side of the road.

She saw a blurry light coming up ahead on her side of the road and decided to stop. The wipers cleared some of the rain and in between Anna could see a shadow, and it was towards her car. She panicked and immediately locked all the doors.

The shadow got closer and closer, but the rain made it impossible to see where it was exactly. Suddenly, she heard a knock on the window on the passenger side next to her. She didn't move. Another knock. Anna held her breath, ready to scream. Then, the shadow tried to open the passenger's side door; they pulled hard a few times and Anna feared they might break the door.

Then she heard a voice. 'Hello? Can you open the door please?' the voice said. It sounded like a woman's voice, but Anna was still unsure. 'Please, can you open?' another knock on the passenger's window. Anna started breathing again slowly; the voice sounded harmless. She opened the door and a black soaking wet woman almost flew in; from the strong wind; and sat down on the passenger's seat. She looked the same age as Anna, only dressed more fashionably.

'What took you so long?' she said and cleared some water of her face. Anna picked a box of tissues from the floor behind her seat and gave it to the woman. She did it without looking at her face. The woman looked like she was mad angry; she breathed heavily and used some of the tissues to dry herself. 'I'm sorry,' she said, calmer but still somewhat cranky. 'My bikes have a flat tire and I got stuck here for almost an hour. And the stupid rain won't stop.'

Anna felt bad about leaving this woman here in the rain. She thought about giving her a ride back to the dorms but then realized she never asked her if she was a student. But before she could say anything, the woman said, 'Just let me stay with you for a while. I mean, if you need to go somewhere then go, I won't bother you. I'll stay in your car. I don't care. Just let me be dry. We can leave the bike here; they're dead anyway.'

Anna shrugged and started the car; this woman was weird. 'I'm Lyla, by the way.' Lyla said and put her hand in front of Anna for a shake. 'I'm Anna, ' Anna said and looked away. 'Not a shaker, I see,' Lyla mentioned and Anna nodded in agreement, still looking away. Then she put the car on 'Drive' and drove off.

Anna looked at the GPS and got confused. The rain was probably blocking the satellite and it made the image on the screen blurry and unreadable. She couldn't see much through the windshield and she didn't know if she was even driving the right way. And thanks to the wind, it was harder to drive since the car was going back and forth from side to side, like a play toy car someone was controlling from afar.

She thought about pulling over on the sidelines when Lyla said, 'I think I see something over there. Can you go that way?'. She was pointing at something far ahead on Anna's left side. Anna couldn't see much herself, but she figured Lyla saw something that could be a traffic sign or a road sign they can use to know where they are.

Anna listened to Lyla's directions and drove to where she was told to. 'Stop!' Lyla raised her voice so loud it made Anna stop the car at once. They both panted and tried to catch their breaths. Anna turned to ask Lyla why she screamed so loud when she noticed what Lyla had been looking at. The wipes ran a little, making it easier to see through the heavy rain. It looked like they stopped 3 feet from the front door of someone's house. The door seemed brand new, and right as they looked at it, it broke from the wind and opened.

# CHAPTER 4

THEY LOOKED AT EACH OTHER, TERRIFIED. LYLA MENTIONED something about a scene from a horror movie, but Anna didn't quite get the joke. She was too busy thinking about how much she didn't want to be there and how much she missed her dried room back at the dorms.

Lyla, on the other hand, was a fierce cookie; she's not one of those girls who would stay sitting around, waiting to be rescued. 'Come on,' she said. 'Let's go inside.' And before Anna could find the words to respond, she opened the door and rushed inside the house, completely ignoring the rain. And even though Anna loved staying alone by herself, she thought it would be wiser to come inside and have a place to dry in. So, she grabbed her phone and rushed inside, after Lyla.

The two were terrified, standing at the front door, though Lyla would never admit she was. The place was pitch dark and they could only see as much as the lightning had allowed them to see every few seconds. Lyla worked up all her courage and screamed at the void, 'Hello? Somebody there? HELLO? ANYBODY HOME?' No response. She shrugged while saying, 'Maybe they left or something.'

Suddenly, they heard a sound coming from above them. They looked at the wooden staircase in front of them and flowed it with their eyes all the way to the second floor. 'Hello?' Lyla tried again. Anna was shaking; she wanted to tell Lyla to shut up and go back to the car. The whole situation didn't feel right to her and she just wanted to go away.

They heard the sound again; this time, it sounded like someone was walking above them. 'Who's there?!' Lyla screamed.

'Who are you?' the voice responded. It sounded like a shaking-defensive sound of a woman.

'Come down and show yourself!' Lyla continued screaming.

'You come up!' the voice squicked. 'I mean...' the voice cleared their throat to sound more threatening, 'you should come upstairs and show yourself to us.'

'Sounds harmless,' Anna thought and the air came back to her lunges. The sounds were now squeaks; like the voice was earlier; and they turned into two shaking young women; probably the same age as Anna and Lyla; as they were coming down the stairs.

A strong thunder shook the house down and all of a sudden, the electricity came back on. Now everybody could finally see every-one. The two young women were now standing in front of them, drenched with water as they were. The first was a short redhead and she had green eyes like Anna's; or maybe they were brighter. The second one was taller, but for an unknown reason, she was hiding behind the short one, and Anna had trouble seeing how she looked like.

'Get off me,' the redhead said and shook off the taller one, pushing her away. Now Anna could fully see the second one and immediately she wished she couldn't. This one looked exactly like Sara did back when Anna first met her. It made Anna want to throw up. This girl had the same blond hair, the same navy-blue eyes, the same height, the same everything. It was too scary to watch. Like Sara had come back into her life, just to haunt her again. But, this version of Sara was drenched to her bones and was wearing wet cheerleader's uniforms.

The only thing that was different between them was the voice.

'I wasn't doing anything!' she squicked. And Anna thought she was probably the one who was screaming at them from the second floor earlier.

Lyla was the first to come back to her senses. 'Who are you two and why are you here?' she tried to look intimidating as she came closer to them. It seemed to be working since the redheaded one took a step back to the staircase.

'We should be asking you that,' said Sara's lookalike and copied Lyla's intimidating behavior.

Maybe it was because she got too scared, or maybe it was something else, but suddenly, the redheaded one blurred, 'I'm Emma.'. Sara's lookalike looked at her like she was a traitor. 'Aaand,' she continued, mumbling, 'this is Samantha.' She pointed at Sara's lookalike like she was confessing a secret.

Lyla smiled for her victory. 'Well, Emma,' she said, taunting. 'It's nice to meet you. I'm Lyla. And Ms. Shocked over there is Anna.' She pointed back at Anna without looking at her. Anna looked away when the others looked at her. 'You two just got here, right?' Lyla continued, taunting them. Emma, still somewhat scared, nodded in obedience. Lyla enjoyed this; maybe too much, and it made Samantha even edgier.

Anna thought about going back to the car and going back to her room when another lightning struck; a loud thunder followed it and they both reminded her the enviable reality. She's stuck here with those girls and the one she's desperately trying to erase. The one that won't leave, even in her dreams after all those years, and now haunts her in real life.

Samantha noticed all the looks Anna had been giving her, unconsciously, but she couldn't quite understand them; something about them annoyed her and she wanted Anna to stop. 'I think we all should dry our clothes,' she said in order to avoid the gaze.

'We saw a fireplace in one of the rooms upstairs.' Emma continued, trying to avoid Lyla's intimidating eyes. 'Do you have something we could use to light up a fire?' Anna and Lyla switched looks between them; they don't. They both nodded their heads 'no'.

The strong wind blew hard and the front door was shut with a bang. All four girls jumped in their place, but Samantha was the only one who screamed. 'I think we should all go upstairs anyway,' Emma suggested in order to calm everybody down. 'At least we'll have a warm place to spend the night.'

The last line made Anna shocked; she immediately retrieved her phone from her jeans' left back pocket and looked at the screen. She blinked a few times, hoping the time would change. It was almost eight p.m. and keeping in mind the heavy rain outside; that by now had turned into a storm; remained her, again, the inability to drive in this weather. Thanks to the dumb book she wanted before, now, she has no choice but to stay here until the stupid storm wears off. She sighed.

Anna turned her head down and followed the other three upstairs to the second floor. This floor seemed bigger than the one below them; but, then again, they didn't spend enough time looking at it. On the second floor they saw three or four doors. The first one on the right was the room Emma had mentioned before. It had two wide beds on both sides of the room, right in front of each other; a makeup table and a full-body mirror right next to the door; and the fireplace was placed at the end of the room, next to a wall of glass windows. They seemed breakable from afar, but as they got closer, they could see how thick those windows really were.

Emma and Samantha each sat on a different bed; Lyla looked through the windows at the storm. And Anna? She was still standing at the door, fighting the instinct to run away. Suddenly, the obvious truth crossed her mind. 'I think we shouldn't touch or move anything,' she said and caught the attention of all the presents in the room. She just realized this was the first thing they all heard her say since she got there.

'So, you CAN speak,' said Samantha. She got off the bed and walked towards Anna. Anna forgot how to breathe for a second; if Emma wouldn't have woken her up, she might have fainted right about now. Instead, Emma said, 'What do you mean?' and Anna came back to her senses.

'I think she means,' Lyla replied instead, since Anna was too busy, carefully scanning the approaching Sara, that is, Samantha, towards her. 'What if the owner decides to come back tonight? It clearly looks like someone still lives here. What if they showed up tonight and see that we made a mess of their house?'

The other two exchanged looks before letting Samantha respond. 'First of all,' she said, full of confidence, leaving no trace of the scared shaking girl from before. 'You need to chill. And second, who in their right mind would go out in this insane weather?' she pointed back at the window. Now, they could see through it flying tree branches, lightning and heavier rain.

'I think,' Samantha continued while looking and walking straight towards Anna. 'We should all explore this place. See what more we can find.' She was now so close to Anna it made her start moving backwards.

'I think Lyla's right.' Emma said, still sitting on the bed. She, now, laid on the bed, not caring about making it wet underneath her. Lyla went back to her window, and they both seemed to ignore Samantha. But Samantha wasn't about to give up that easily; she wanted to explore this place even if it meant she'll have to do it alone and by herself.

Just now, she noticed Anna was looking at her strangely again, as if she was scared of her, and Samantha was going to take advantage of that. She kept walking toward Anna, forcing her to walk backwards, until they both got out of the room. Once they were both out, Samantha simply shrugged and went down the stairs, back to the first floor; as if she was telling Anna she doesn't give a damn about her.

Anna went back inside the room. The other two were busy doing what they did before, and Anna had no choice but to do the same. She sat at the other bed, crossed her legs, and waited for the sun to come out.

# CHAPTER 5

AN HOUR, OR MAYBE MORE, HAD PASSED SINCE SAMANTHA WENT to explore the house. But it felt like five minutes to Lyla who was still staring at the storm. It all looked the same to her and she didn't notice the time went by. Suddenly, she saw a flickering light in the dark outside. The light turned into two lights, and they grew bigger as they got closer to them. Now, she was able to see the car that was approaching the house.

'Hey, girls...' she said, raising her voice, not realizing she was waking up Emma and Anna, which both fell asleep on their beds. 'What... what happened?' mumbled sleepy Emma, as she got up and sat on her bed. Lyla immediately 'shh'ed her and Emma looked at her, confused.

Anna, as opposed to sleepy Emma, was only dowsing off before; and now she jumped up all at once and stood up on both feet. She got angry at herself for letting herself go like that and fall asleep. She'll be more careful from now on.

'What happened?' Anna asked and approached the window. Her whole body was getting ready for danger. The window, huge as it was, had no curtains whatsoever, which made it impossible for the two to hide themselves from the shadows leaving the car. And, the fact they now had electricity, and the lights were on, wasn't much help. Lyla did the same 'shh' for Anna and they both looked outside.

Emma, who finally managed to pull herself off the bed, walked to the window and asked, 'What's going on?'. Both Anna and Lyla 'shh'ed her at the same time, which made Emma panic and cover her mouth with her hands. Lyla pointed at the window and the three of them looked through it.

Four shadows left the car beneath them and three of them rushed to the door, leaving one of them to stop for a second. For a moment it seemed it was looking at girls. Strong lightning lit up the sky and the three could see a vague image of a man; that, now, they knew for sure, was looking at them.

They heard a sound coming from downstairs; the door opened and then was shut. They turned around together and looked at the open door. Then, they heard the steps coming up the stairs. Anna closed her eyes; Emma, still covering her mouth, was ready to scream, and Lyla? She was busy trying to find a sharp object to use as a weapon. After a quick scan of the room, she found an iron stick next to the fireplace and held it up behind her like a bat, ready to swing.

The steps got louder and louder as the four shadows went up the stairs. This bizarre situation made Anna start to have flash-backs. HE came to mind. She kept thinking about how he'll enter the room, any second now, and her heart beat like crazy. She stopped breathing for a while. The tears streamed by themselves, even though her eyes were too wide open, in the fear he'll actually come in right now. He and the other teachers, that is…

The four shadows finally stood at the opened door and the three girls froze in their place. Four drenched men stood in front of them, wearing jeans and t-shirts with open jackets on them, looking like a well-dressed boy band. Emma was the first to come back to her senses. 'I'm Em-' she started, smiling, when Lyla grabbed her hand and pulled her behind.

'What are you doing?' she whispered back to the shocked Emma. 'We don't know them. They could be dangerous.'

One of the four men, a blond, blue-eyed boy, took a step toward Lyla and said, taunting, 'Ohh... do I scare you, little girl?' The other three men looked amused. The tall black one and the brown-haired one started laughing; but, the fourth one seemed to slowly drift from the conversation. Something had definitely caught his eye.

Lyla felt her blood boiling with anger. 'Who are you calling 'little girl'?' she was about to hit him with the bet; that is the iron stick thingy, but Emma stopped her at the last minute. 'I don't think it's a good idea,' she said.

'I don't care what you think,' Lyla protested while trying to get the bet back.

'What's wrong, little girl? Are you scared?' he said, taunting again. The blond blue-eyed one laughed and grinned. It made Lyla even madder and she left the bet at Emma, and turned to hit him with her bear hands. Emma quickly ran between them and literally was the only thing kipping Lyla from punching him in the face.

Anna's breath returned to her body all at once, and her body lost all balance. She fell, sitting down, next to the window. Her hands held her head from reaching her knees and hitting them. She sighed two or three times, quietly, trying to make the tears stop. The fourth one, a tall mocha-skinned boy, looked at her from the door. He had no idea what was going on, but somehow, he wanted to help this shaken-looking girl. She reminded him of someone else he once knew.

The only thing that could put an end to this absurd situation was nothing other than the long-awaited return of Samantha; and she did it the way only she could. She pushed through the four men, ignoring them completely and making room for herself to come in. when she was finally standing inside, everybody could see that she was holding two bottles of wine.

'What are you doing?' Lyla yelled at her, looking at the wine. Samantha opened her mouth to answer when she heard a man's voice behind her calling her, 'Babe!'. Samantha turned around and her eyes lit up with joy. 'Baby!' she screamed and rushed to hug the brown-haired one, ignoring Lyla completely, and still she managed somehow to keep the wine bottles unharmed.

'What are you doing here?' they both said at the same time, to each other. Samantha and her boyfriend were one of those couples who read each other's minds and talked at the same time, all the time. It was quite annoying. 'It's a long story!' they both replied at the same time again and laughed.

Samantha turned back to the girls and said proudly, 'Girls, this is my boyfriend, David'. The brown-haired one, that Samantha just hugged, raised his hand; proudly. It was clear they both just wanted to show off. Emma and Lyla exchanged looks but then decided not to care. They went back to the beds.

Since she didn't get the attention she wanted, Samantha kept talking. 'This is Bryan, ' she pointed at the blond, blue-eyed one. 'He's David's roommate.' David looked at Bryan, smiling, only Bryan was too busy trying to catch Lyla's attention again. David seemed hurt by this, for a second, while Lyla, on the other hand, didn't care much.

'This is Andre, ' Samantha introduced the tall black man. Now, she managed to catch Emma's attention. 'He's in David's basketball team.' It was clear that she was still trying to brag, only no one was willing to give her the satisfaction of carrying.

Instead, Emma got off the bed and rushed to shake Andre's hand. It was too tight. 'Hi,' she said. 'I'm Emma. And the violent one on the bed there is Lyla.' When she heard her name, Lyla looked at grinning Bryan, and it made her even madder than she was before. She gave Emma the 'you're a traitor' look; the same one Samantha had given her earlier that night. But Emma was too busy trying to catch Andre's attention then to notice Lyla. She was still holding his hand; too tight.

'What about you?' said the tall mocha-skinned one and looked at Anna. 'Oh,' answered Emma, instead. 'This is Anna, but she doesn't talk much'. The tall mocha-skinned man started walking toward Anna when someone grabbed his sleeve and made him stop. 'Don't waste time on her, Adrian,' Samantha said and placed her arm on his shoulder. 'She's not worth it.' She gave Anna the best 'watch for yourself' look she could give and turned Adrian toward the bed.

Emma just realized something. 'We should call the police or something,' she said. 'Maybe someone will come to rescue us from here.'

'Rescue?' Lyla grinned. 'What are you? a freakkin' princess or something?'

'No, I,' Emma tried to reply but was cut off by Samantha. 'Does anyone have a phone on you?' she talked to the whole room. They all pulled their phones out and presented them to her. 'Quick, everyone! Look for a signal!' she said. She made them walk around the room and look for a signal that was nowhere to be found.

'I can't find any,' said Bryan and looked at the rest; Emma and Adrian nodded in agreement. 'Babe, I'm sorry,' said David. 'I can't find one either.'

That should have been enough to silence her up, but Samantha wasn't about to give up. It's not the phones or the 'being found' thing that she wasn't giving up on; it was the attention. So, she came up with an idea instead. 'Everybody, sit down on the floor,' she said and waved the wine high. 'Let's play a game.' When she said the last line, it made Anna raise her head and her eyes filled with horror.

# CHAPTER 6

SAMANTHA FORCED EVERYBODY TO SIT ON THE FLOOR IN A circle. They all opposed it, of course, but the only one who actually fought her, demanding not to participate, was Lyla. She pulled away and pushed Samantha a few times, but since Samantha wasn't about to give up so easily, and was stronger than she looked, in the end, Lyla was pulled and forced to sit down with the rest.

Once they all finally sat down, all but Anna, that is; Samantha gave one bottle to David and the other to Bryan. 'But, babe,' David said. 'How are we going to open them?' she smiled and picked her skirt's back pocket. She retrieved a small wine opener and showed it to the room proudly, like she just won a trophy. David was the only one who cared to share the excitement and clapped his hands for her.

'I don't think it's a good idea, Samantha,' Emma said and looked worried.

'Yeah, not a good idea,' said Andre and nodded in agreement. Emma's face turned to him, blushing, all at once. It was the first time she heard him say anything; since the minute he walked in; and his voice wormed her body, all over.

Bryan then joined the conversation. 'What if the person who

owns this place finds out we were here?' he said and looked at all of them for answers.

Lyla got up and screamed, 'You're an idiot. You're going to get us all arrested', at Samantha. But Samantha acted like she didn't care at all and rolled her eyes, pushing Lyla back to sit her down.

'Come on, you guys,' Samantha said. 'We're all drenched, cold and stuck here. At least let's have some fun and forget about how we ended up here. And besides, if the owner finds out about us, then we'll explain to them. I'm sure they would understand.' No one believed that Samantha's plan to talk to the owner would work, but she was right about one thing: They all wanted to have fun and forget the misfortunes that got them there. So they all agreed to play the game.

While she was talking, Samantha took the bottle that she gave Bryan earlier and opened it. She was holding it the entire time she was talking, but the second she was done, the unexpected happened. Anna, who was crying at the window all this time, got up, walked up to her and snatched Samantha's opened bottle from her hand. She drank the wine like it was water, making everybody around her shocked.

'Hi!' Samantha acted offended. 'That was mine.' David pulled her skirt down a bit to get her attention; once he did, he gave her back the bottle she let him hold earlier and they both smiled.

No one expected Anna to sit down when she did. She joined the circle, sitting between Bryan and Adrian, and didn't say a word; she just kept on drinking quietly. Samantha tried to catch her eyes but couldn't. Anna had completely closed herself up.

'So,' Lyla said, trying to clear the heavy vibes in the room. 'Why are we sitting on the floor again?' Samantha sat down between David and Bryan and said, 'The rules of this game are simple. You spin the bottle, and whomever the bottle hits on, have to kiss each other. If you don't, you have to drink.'

'Come on, Samantha,' said Lyla. 'That's lame.'

'Yeah!' agreed Emma. 'This isn't junior high, you know...'

'And besides,' Bryan looked at the bottle Samantha just opened. 'There's no way THAT would be enough for all of us.'

'That's why I brought two,' she stared angrily at Anna, who just finished the whole bottle by herself. Nevertheless, she didn't seem bothered by Samantha's words.

'Hey,' David said, defensive. 'It's not like we have something else to do here.' The rest of them exchanged their looks between them. They might not have wanted to admit it, but he had a point. Looking at the window, all at the same time, they realized it all together. The truth was that they are all stuck here, in this place, until the morning; at least, if not more.

'So, let's play,' said Andre, with his deep voice. Emma clanged on his arm and hugged him tightly. Maybe he felt uncomfortable, but Andre didn't seem to show it. He just kept on sitting there while being hugged by a much shorter redhead person.

'Ok then,' Samantha said, reaching her hand and waiting for Anna to give her the empty bottle. Anna gave her the bottle without lifting her eyes from the ground.

This was too painful for her. Anna felt as if she was on camera on one of those pranks shows on TV; only, this wasn't funny. She kept having flashbacks that filled up her mind. And all of her emotions, she felt back then, came back to her at once. She could feel the pain, the shame, the sadness, and the will to flee the scene all over again. But the storm outside made the last one impossible to execute.

Once she held the bottle in her hand, Samantha smiled and placed it in the middle of the circle. 'So, who wants to go first?' she said and waited for a volunteer.

'Ugh,' sighed Lyla. 'I'll do it.' She lifted her eyes for a second and saw Bryan's amused look. 'What are YOU looking at?' she raised her voice and was about to punch his face again. Emma stopped her at the last minute, again.

'Let's just play. Ok?' Emma tried to calm her down while slowly taking her hand back to the bottle on the ground.

When she finally calmed down, Lyla spun the bottle, and it landed on Samantha. They both didn't like it at the same time but reacted differently: Lyla got up and announced that she wouldn't play anymore, while Samantha crossed her hands on her chest and turned her head in content. Andre reminded them of the rules: they could drink the wine if they don't want to kiss. While David and Bryan openly opposed it, Lyla and Samantha were thankful for the opportunity to escape and were ready to drink from the bottle.

'So, if every time we spin the bottle and it'll land on someone we don't want to, and we'll just drink; we'll run out of wine too soon and this won't be fun,' Emma made her point.

'But...' Samantha tried to resist, but it was pointless; they all already agreed to it. Lyla and Samantha, both took a quick and small sip of the wine to get themselves mentally ready. Due to the fact they sat in front of each other, at the circle, they had to pull closer to each other before they kissed. It lasted for no longer than a second, and still, unexpectedly, they both felt warm, flustered and shy after it; but they would never admit it.

'Samantha, now it's your turn.' Bryan has woken both of them from their inner feelings and brought them back to the game. Samantha spun the bottle and it landed on Andre. She shrugged and pulled herself closer to him. It made Emma angry for some reason. Samantha kissed him longer than she kissed Lyla, and now David got upset. He cleared his throat loudly so they would get the point and stop, and so they did.

Now, it was Andre's turn to spin the bottle and it landed on Bryan; it made both of them turn red all over. For some reason Bryan looked at David and not at Lyla when the bottle landed on him. Was he waiting for David's approval? Anyway, both Andre and Bryan took a sip of the wine before they had to do it.

The whole group kept on playing for at least half an hour before it was Adrian's turn to spin the bottle. At the last round Emma kissed him and it meant that now it was his turn to do it. For the first time since they started to play, the bottle landed on Anna.

Up until now Anna was quietly sitting by the circle, not moving or commenting on anything. She was too busy trying to quiet down the noises inside her brain. THE DEAN's voice, his smell and his gentle but evil smile haunted her mind and left no room for the reality outside. The last five years of blocking every detail behind a giant wall inside her, started to crumble right in front of her eyes. The worst thing was, she had no idea how to make it stop.

So, that second when Samantha had declared, happily, that Adrian had to kiss her, Anna heard it from far, far away. She lifted her head slowly and scanned the room. Maybe it was the wine, but it sounded like Sara's voice had climbed inside Samantha's body, which was already a creepy replica of Sara' body, and now it was like she was right there in front of her, still making her play this stupid game.

Adrian turned to her. 'You don't have to if you don't want to.' He said and looked at her eyes; they seemed dark and dead, even though they had the greenest eye color he had ever seen in his life. But, before he knew what was going on, Anna had already kissed him. Just like that. At first, he was shocked; but slowly he let himself go. There was something different about her kiss that he never felt before, with anyone else; Her lips tasted like wine and something else, but he couldn't get exactly what.

The rest of the group seemed baffled by the situation. Of course, they all wanted Anna to participate; all but Samantha, that is; but they were also shocked by how fast she got from not being in the room to fully kissing Adrian passionately. She was weird and mysterious, all at the same time. Like a puzzle they weren't sure they wanted to solve.

When the kiss ended, Anna pulled back. She couldn't bear looking into Adrian's eyes. Instead, she grabbed the second bottle, which by now was half-way full, and finished it all. She didn't even hear the rest of the group protesting against her, not to do it.

Adrian, on the other end, was blushing. It wasn't something he was used to, since the last time it happened to him was back when he was 14 and had his first kiss. He got up and sat on the bed. That was everybody's cue that the game was over.

Emma suggested she would go and get more wine. She was still holding Andre's arm, which meant he had to come with her. Samantha pointed to the fact that she was the only one who knew where the wine cellar was, so she should be the one to go there. Lyla got angry at the both of them and yelled that they shouldn't mess with the things in this house so much, but they both ignored her.

Samantha and Emma got up, forced David and Andre to join them, and left the room, going down. Lyla got so mad no one was listening to her that she left the room; one the opposite direction, going up. Bryan followed her upstairs, even though she clearly said, a number of times, she didn't want him to.

Adrian was still catching his breath when he realized he and Anna were the only ones left in the room. He was feeling too much of his body reacting to this girl, and he wanted some answers why. He got up, sat on the floor on his knees and touched Anna's shoulder; she didn't move. He was about to do it again, but then she turned her face back at him. She didn't say anything; she just stared at his lips.

He couldn't resist it anymore. He held the back of her neck and pulled her toward him, forcing their lips to meet. Once they did, he was certain she was definitely kissing him back. They got up and stood while kissing each other passionately. His hands lowered to her back and he was about to hug her, but then she suddenly stopped.

At first, her eyes stared at the ground; but after a few seconds, it seemed she worked up enough courage to look at him. Her eyes still looked dark and somewhat dead, but they were also very drunk. He thought about stopping completely since it wouldn't be right to kiss someone when they're drunk. But, what was he supposed to do, when that drunk someone was kissing him on her own? And she wasn't going to stop.

Before he realized what was going on, Adrian's jacket and shirt were lying on the ground and his jeans were unbuttoned. Anna took off her own jacket, then put his hands on her waist and lifted them up, showing him she wanted him to take off her sweater. After he did, he held her body close to him and turned them both toward the bed. Anna fell on the bed and immediately tried to take her jeans off. Adrian did the same for himself; only he was still standing up.

Anna couldn't say much about where her mind was at that

moment. The wine, the thoughts in her head and the warm and sweet body she felt against her own, were all mixed together. All she knew was that every time she looked at this guy, and his grey-blue eyes looked back at her, it made her want to tear off his clothes and make him her own.

He climbed on the bed while kissing her legs slowly. It made her heart beat too fast and her face blush even more. She sat up, held his head and directed him to kiss her. She was in full control and showed him what she wanted; he wasn't used to it, but he liked it.

They rolled over a few times while they kissed. When she was on top of him, he worked up the courage and opened her bra. It made her stop and look at him. She gulped her saliva and stared at him, shocked, for a second. He wanted to say he was sorry, since she somehow seemed angry at him, but then... the unexpected happened.

Anna took off her underwear all at once and then she did the same for Adrian. He tried to sit up and help her, but she pushed him back down. She climbed on top of him, putting him inside of her, and started moving. Adrian froze in his place. This outrageously beautiful woman was riding on top of him, making him feel the most incredible feeling he had in a while; but at the same time she closed her eyes, and it seemed like she was a thousand worlds away. It triggered something inside of him, something he didn't like at all.

Anna heard breathing sounds around her. At first, they were far away, but slowly they became closer and closer and louder and louder. She opened her eyes and looked at the man underneath her. She noticed, only now, that she had been holding his arms against his chest, not allowing him to move an inch, and she let them go at once. He immediately held her waist, so she wouldn't fall off. She could see the red marks she left on his arms.

Looking at his face made her realize the sounds she heard weren't coming from him, and still, she heard them quite close. While they kept on moving each other, it slowly came to her mind that those sounds were coming from her. The second she realized it, she instantly stopped, covered her mouth with both her hands and held her breath.

'What's wrong?' Adrian sat up, still holding her body from falling off. 'Do you want to stop?' he said, worried; she clearly wasn't ok. She nodded her head 'no' while still covering her mouth and holding her breath. In an instinct he pulled her in and hugged her, holding her body tightly against his chest. All the air in her lungs finally broke her lips and went out, like a balloon being slowly let go.

She had no idea how he knew what she needed; at that moment, or why she needed him to do it. She was just thankful he did, but she also couldn't tell him anything. Her mind was no longer inside this room. She clenched her head against Adrian's chest and closed her eyes. Her mind filled up with the same images, repeating themselves endlessly. And all she could hear was, 'Good cats don't 'meow' at their owners; unless they are told to'. Over and over again. An endless loop of it.

# CHAPTER 7

WHILE THIS WAS HAPPENING UPSTAIRS, SAMANTHA, EMMA, David, and Andre went down to the wine cellar. This room, or maybe it's best to call it, wing, was all made of wood. The walls, the floor, and also the ceiling were made of this dark-brown wood. On the walls, the wooden shelves held an enormous collection of wines; that made Emma wonder who lived here and why in the world they left.

'This way,' Samantha said and led them to the middle of the room. 'Choose,' she said and raised her arms, presenting the room like she owned it. David and Andre didn't wait for her to tell them to; they already searched the shelves and looked at the different kinds of wine. She made a face and put her hands on both sides of her waist.

At the back of the room there was a table covered with a see-through glass. Inside, it had more wine openers in different colors and sizes. Samantha went to the table, lifted the glass cover and put the wine opener she took before, back inside. To replace it, she took another wine opener, a bigger one, made of white gold.

Emma still stood at the door. It crossed her mind that this all was a very bad idea. 'How on earth are we going to explain this to the owner when they'll get back?' she thought. She refused to get inside when they all did, but now she realized she was the only one left there by herself. And the fear of being alone in this place made her rush in to find the others.

When Emma finally found them, they all sat on the floor. David and Andre had already picked a bottle each, and Samantha was busy opening them. They all exchanged looks when she sat down, but no one said anything about it. To break the silence, Samantha suggested they would play TRUTH OR DARE. They all protested together, saying they had enough games for one night. Instead, they decided to have a calm conversation over wine.

'So, how did you two end up here?' David asked, looking at the girls, trying to start the conversation. 'The last time I saw you,' he turned to Samantha. 'You were at the game.'

He was referring to the basketball game they all attended, at the college gym, much earlier that day. David and Andre were playing while Samantha was on the sidelines, cheering. As the head cheerleader; and the only one on the team with a cheerleading scholarship, she had twice the responsibilities than anyone else on her team. Once the game ended, and the players and cheerleaders went to the showers, Samantha stayed behind to lock up the equipment like she always did.

By the time she was done, it was already late in the afternoon. The storm outside was raging as she went inside her car. It was impossible to see anything in that weather, let alone drive in it. She swore, she never saw her coming until it was almost too late. Emma gave her a doubtful look and an angry one at the same time.

'You ran her over?' David said shocked and took a sip from the wine.

'No! not really,' Samantha defended. She hit a street light pole, as she tried to avoid hitting Emma, the second she saw her. 'And besides,' she added, 'who goes out jogging in this weather, anyway?!' She returned Emma's looks back to her. She took a few sips of the wine to calm herself down.

'I wasn't jogging, I was running. I was late to my practice and I had to run there.' Emma corrected her, and it made Samantha silently mumble, 'Take a bus, you weirdo,' to herself.

'You had a practice? Doing what?' David asked, and both him and Andre seemed interested to know.

'I'm a gymnast,' she smiled and the three of them looked at her, confused.

Meanwhile, at another part of the house, at the third floor to be exact, Lyla was trying to avoid Bryan. He kept following her, asking her questions, even though she specifically told him not to, for more than once.

She finally lost her calm, tuned back at him and yelled, 'Will you please shut up already?!' he stopped and looked at her, grinning. 'Go away!' she kept on yelling at him.

'Wait,' he tried to warn her, but it was already too late. She turned back her way but missed the fact she stopped earlier right in front of a shut door. She now bumped her head into the door, fell back into his arms and they both fell on the ground.

'AW!' she yelled at him like it was his fault they fell. She sat up, looked back at him and her anger disappeared in a second; he looked like he was in pain. 'Are you ok?' she asked. He held his stomach, on the right side, as he sat up. When she fell on him, she did it with her elbow first and it hit him right at the stomach as he hit the ground.

'I'm fine,' he said, 'It's because you're so heavy.' He tried to tease her, and make her angry again; and he almost did, but then the pain came back, and it was hard for him to keep laughing; and hard for her to get mad.

'What can I do to help you?' she said, worried. That gentle side of her surprised him and he almost blushed.

'I don't know,' he said, keeping his hands on his stomach. 'Tell me something.'

'Like what?' she asked and got closer to him. The pain was too much and he had to raise his voice when he said, 'I don't know, ok?!'

She pulled back. 'Don't yell at me!' she screamed.

He forced himself to calm down in spite of the pain. 'AW! just..

anything… keep my mind off this, AW! pain.' He seemed to be really hurt.

'Ok, ok!' she yelled back; this time she was worried and not angry, but still… 'You want to know how I ended up here tonight?' she asked and he nodded slowly.

'Yeah, sure,' he said. 'Well…' she said and then stopped to think about where to start. 'Lyla!' he yelled at her, waking her from her thoughts. 'Ok! ok!' she yelled back.

So she told him about how this morning, she still had a boyfriend; but, it didn't last until lunch. She went to his room, first thing in the morning, to surprise him, just being a good girlfriend and all. But, when she knocked, he didn't answer. He also didn't reply to her calls or texts. It was unusual of him, so she opened the door; just to make sure he was ok.

'So, this idiot cheated on you, right?' Bryan filled the rest. She nodded, her eyes full of raging anger and fire. 'This sucks,' he said. The gentle way he said that made her calm for some reason. 'Thanks,' she said, smiling back.

After that, the stupid storm destroyed her car and it didn't start. So, she had to commute all day with her friend's bike. She took a wrong turn on her way to the store and got lost in the rain. She tried to keep on cycling, when she had a flat tire in the middle of the road. 'I swear,' she said. 'If that girl' she meant Anna, 'Hadn't stopped her car for me, I'd probably be dead in the rain by now.'

For some reason, her story made Bryan feel much better about himself, and the pain in his stomach slowly drifted away. He smiled and said she was probably being possessed by bad luck or something. 'I better not come near you. I might catch it from you,' he teased again.

'Get lost!' she said, angry, making him grin again. She got up and started walking.

'Wait!' he said behind her, struggling to stand up. 'Help me get up.'

'Fwe…' she thought. 'That's a proof you're ok,' and she smiled secretly to herself as she went on exploring the rest of the house.

# CHAPTER 8

ANNA FOUND HERSELF STANDING IN THE ROOM, BY HERSELF. IT
was pitch dark and had zero light inside. Until HE walked in and
turned them on. 'Come here, Kitty,' he said. She walked in but then
he grabbed her arm and pulled her back to him. 'Cats don't walk
like humans do, Kitty,' he corrected her and pushed her head down
so she would go on all four limbs. 'Good Kitty,' he praised her and
petted her head. 'Now, go on, come in,' he continued. The room
was the size of a shoe box, and it contained a single bed, a chair,
and a small light, hanging from the ceiling.

Now it was his turn to enter the room. He sat comfortably on
the chair and looked at her, grinning. 'Come here, Kitty,' he used
the voice people sometimes make when they talk to babies or their
pets. She was about to get up and walk to him like she was used to,
but he 'ticked' his tongue at her. She realized he wanted her to act
like a cat, and she didn't want to; but, she also didn't have much
choice, considering what happened to the last kid who said 'no'
to HIM.

She went down on all fours and walked like a cat toward the
chair. When she got to him, he petted her head and face like a cat.
'Cats lick themselves, Kitty,' he said with that tone she never heard

before. She gulped her saliva before she stuck her tongue out and turned to lick her arm. 'A-a, Kitty,' he looked at her uniform, 'cats don't wear clothes.'

Anna started to shake. He pulled her up, took off her uniform and her underwear, and pushed her back to the floor. He cleared his throat to remind her of his last request. She stared at the ground, fighting the tears; then, since she had no choice, she stuck her tongue out and licked her arms. Then, she licked her shoulders and looked at him. 'Good Kitty,' he praised her again.

'Cats also lick their owners,' he said with that look again. That crazy-looking, somewhat happy look in his eyes. He got up, opened his belt, and pulled his pants and underwear down. He grabbed Anna's neck and pulled her close to him. He forced her to open her mouth and then he forced himself inside.

Anna felt like she couldn't breathe. It was choking her up, making her eyes tear up and her nose to run out. Unconsciously, she made sounds with her mouth while she was choking. Suddenly, he grabbed her head and threw her to the ground. He looked at her from above and said, 'Good cats don't 'meow' at their owners, Kitty; unless they are told to.'

He forced himself inside her body and said that line repeatedly until he was finished with her. By the time he was done, Anna had silenced herself completely, telling herself she was nothing but a cat and 'good cats don't 'meow' at their owners; unless they are told to.' That line kept echoing her mind over and over again.

# CHAPTER 9

ANNA WOKE UP SCREAMING; AGAIN. LIGHTNING FLASHED ON HER face, followed by a strong thunder. It seemed like she was waking up like it was any other morning; only this time it was slightly different. This nightmare was full of much deeper memories than the ones she was used to seeing in her dreams. She couldn't come up with the reason why it suddenly changed, since the words and the images she just experienced in her dream stayed with her; even though she was fully awake now. She tried to wipe the tears from her eyes, but they kept on coming; so she just gave up and let them go.

Suddenly, she found herself in a big bed she couldn't recognize, and the tears immediately stopped. She looked at herself, realized she was naked under the sheets, and instantly turned red. Then, she raised her head and scanned the room, trying to figure out where she was. Sudden pain in her head forced her to grab it tightly, using both her hands. Closing her eyes and holding her aching head, forced her to be reminded about last night. She vaguely recalled the wine and the game, and the immediate images sent chills down her spine.

Then, the reason why she was nacked finally came back to her.

That made her even more redder than before. She recalled how fast their clothes were off and how fast they made it to the bed. She remembered covering her mouth with her hands and his hug, his warm, relaxing hug. It was too much for her; when it happened, and she broke free from it. What happened next was that she pushed him back on the bed, inserted him inside her and moved even faster than she did before.

That feeling she got, her whole body felt it, like exploding from the inside out; in a good, fun, liberating kind of way. And what's even more confusing was the fact that it didn't, not even a little, hurt. She wondered why it didn't hurt when she inserted him inside of her. Wasn't the pain a mandatory, in those kinds of things? Or maybe it wasn't there because she was drunk? Maybe she just fell asleep afterwards? or maybe something else happened? she gasped in panic.

Her thoughts got disturbed by another thunder. This one seemed to be a lot closer than the last one. 'Shit,' she thought and held her head, using one hand. She just realized she was missing classes that she would have to find a way to make up for. She probably would have kept scolding herself, if the reason for why she was in this bed nacked, wouldn't have come into the room right now.

'Hey,' he said, smiling. She looked at him, standing at the door, but then immediately looked away. He wasn't wearing a shirt and it made Anna blush. 'Are you ok?' he kept talking to her while walking toward the bed.

The second he sat on it, she jumped to the floor, taking the blanket with her. 'Can you please put a shirt on?' she said without taking her eyes off the ground.

He found this girl very amusing. 'It didn't bother you last night,' he thought while looking at her face turning redder and redder. He had to bite his lips a bit in order to keep himself from grinning too much. He got off the bed and picked his shirt off the floor. 'Thank you,' she sighed, relieved.

He went back to sit on the bed and said, 'The others are downstairs,' he lifted his thumb and pointed above and behind his shoulder, back at the door. 'Having breakfast. David found the kitchen last night, and apparently, there's a lot of food there. You looked like you were having a deep sleep, so I didn't want to wake you. I came back to check on you-'

'Thanks,' she interrupted him. 'I'm fine,' she said, trying to make him leave.

'I see,' he said, still amused. 'Well,' he got up and turned to the door. 'I'll be downstairs with the others if you'll decide to join us.'

He started walking to the door when she suddenly said, 'About last night.' He immediately turned back to her. 'I...' she started saying but couldn't keep her face off the floor.

'It felt good, didn't it?' he smiled, and her heart started beating like crazy. He walked up to her, lifted her head, and looked right into her eyes. 'I definitely would want to do it again with you,' he grinned and then added, 'If you want to.'

She removed his hand and suddenly went back to her walled-up self. 'You can leave now and go back to the others.' She pointed to the door. 'I want to get dressed.' She referred to her clothes on the floor.

'Go ahead,' he said, bit his lips again in order not to grin too much, and left her alone with her thoughts. Anna starred at the open door and had the sudden urge to follow him downstairs. It scared her; she never had such an urge before and she had no idea what to do.

So instead, she turned to the floor and lifted her underwear. After she wore them, she picked up her jeans and discovered her phone lying on the ground beneath them. She assumed it fell off her back pocket when she threw the jeans on the ground, right before they... She couldn't think about it without turning red. So instead, she'll come up with a distraction.

She needed to take a shower. She desperately wanted to wash off last night from her body and her mind. She wore the rest of her clothes and went out, searched the floor looking for a bathroom, and not so far from the room she slept in, she found one. More like a royal one. The room was too wide, and it could contain a large number of people in it. The bathtub was round, like a clear white jacuzzi and could fit at least two or three people at the same time.

Anna felt it was too much to use such a fancy place, just to take a simple shower. She felt more of a nothing than before, just looking at it. But smelling her body odor made it clear she had no other choice. She opened the tap and the bottom of the bathtub closed on it's own, in order to fill it up. She sighed and got inside. She was definitely going to be in trouble for this.

She sat in the warm water and wondered what was happening to her. She felt like she was going crazy while trying so hard to keep her emotions in order. 'I'm fine,' she told herself, trying to sound as convincing as possible, 'I'm fine.'

# CHAPTER 10

WHEN ANNA FINALLY DECIDED TO COME DOWN, IT WAS CLOSER
to lunch time, than it was to breakfast. Lyla and Adrian sat on the
couch in a small living room, not far from the staircase, and looked
through the window. They looked like they were watching TV
when in fact, they were staring at the storm outside. They didn't
even notice her when she sat on the couch right next to them.

Emma walked in. She was about to say something, but then she
noticed Anna. 'How do you feel?' she asked. Her tone sounded
worried, like Anna was sick or something. Her body language said
the same. But, Anna had no mental strength nor the will to start an
argument; so, she forced a smile instead.

Now, Lyla and Andre suddenly noticed her. They both looked
at her with weird looks, like they had something on their minds but
not the guts to say them out loud. But before she had the chance to
say something about it, David, Samantha and Bryan walked in.
David was in the middle of a sentence, teasing, to the other two,
about Emma, who got lost looking for the others. He asked her
earlier to call them to the kitchen for lunch, but it took her way too
much time to do it.

They all stopped at once and looked at her; actually, it was more of a stare than a look. Five people stared at her from different angles, around the room, surrounding her. She felt like she was being surrounded by a firing squad. It got her thinking; Adrian must have told them about last night. When the actual thought came to mind, deeper feelings of humiliation and anger aroused in her, growing more by the second. By the time he finally walked in, she was more than ready to give him an earful.

He opened his mouth to say something and immediately regretted it. 'How dare you?!' she screamed and got them all startled. She stood up and turned to face him. 'What makes you think you have the right?! Who do you think you are?!' she walked up to him, her voice getting louder and louder.

Even though she didn't give him the chance to defend himself, for some unknown reason, he wasn't getting angry at her, not at all. He found her amusing, funny, sexy, and beautiful; and that angry side of her just made him even more sure about his thoughts. But, most of all, she was interesting, in his eyes, like a puzzle he just had to solve.

She kept on screaming at him for more than ten minutes, when Emma suddenly interrupted her. 'Hey, guys…' she pointed at the window. The impossible has happened. Nothing but sunny clear blue sky that made the window look like an oil painting on the wall. And to be even more taunting, the sun sent rays that reached inside the room and warmed it. So absurd it felt like a scene in a cartoon movie.

Anna pulled herself together and seized her chance. She walked back to the main door, opened it and stormed out. Just like that. She wasn't going to spend another minute with those strangers, sitting there, being gossiped and humiliated by them.

She walked inside her car, only to discover she left her car keys at the ignition. She was in a lot of hurry when she left her car last night. She was lucky. 'Thank god nothing happened to the car,' she thought. If it had, it was another unfortunate thing she needed to handle right now. She sighed and rested her head down on her hands.

She sat there for a minute, closing her eyes and keeping her head against the wheel. Who was she yelling at, back there? Him or herself? Was she really mad at Adrian? or was it someone else? Can she even say HIS name? or was it too painful she couldn't breathe? She shook her head and tried to keep her emotions away. She has no time for this; she has more important things to do right now. She started the car, put it on 'drive' and drove off.

On her way back to her dorm, the group she left back at the house, came to her mind. Luckily, there's no chance for them to ever meet again. They know absolutely nothing about her, which meant there was no way for them to come across each other; ever again. Except for him. There was something about Adrian she just couldn't shake off her mind.

When she finally got to her dorm, she stormed in and hugged her bed. Lily looked at her like she was insane. She was wearing her headphones again, so the whole situation lacked context and didn't make sense to her. Lily shrugged and left the room; her roommate was weird like that and there wasn't something she could do about it.

Anna didn't mind that Lily didn't notice her being gone last night. On the contrary, she was actually happy about it. The fewer questions, the better. Luckily, Lily wasn't one of those people to ask questions on questionable things; and Anna preferred it like that.

She got off the bed and went to her desk; her beloved desk. She opened a random book from her endless pile of books and started reading it. There's nothing like a good book to shut the world away. Pure happiness.

# CHAPTER 11

THE DOOR OPENED AGAIN. THIS TIME HE STOOD OUTSIDE. TWO
people walked in, but Anna couldn't see their faces. She was lying
on the floor again, on all four limbs. She only knew they were a
man and a woman, based on their shoes. 'Did you miss me?' the
woman spoke.

Anna's eyes opened widely as she recognized HER voice. She
raised her head and looked at them. Anna had no idea how long it's
been since she last saw the two of them; it felt like ages ago. And
yet, she wasn't exactly happy about the sudden reunion.

Anna tried to say something, but her voice betrayed her and she
couldn't speak; she hasn't used it for a long time. The man and the
woman walked in and up to her, standing close; too close; to her
face. 'You look good, kid,' the man touched her face. His touch
burned Anna's cheek like it was pure fire.

'Adam and I really missed you,' the woman said, 'Aren't you
happy to see us?' She sounded worried, but Anna wasn't buying
her fake emotions anymore.

'Sara asked you a question, Kitty,' HE said from outside. She
hadn't realized, until now, that he was standing there, watching, all

this time. Anna nodded slowly in agreement. She knew she had to obey. She hated herself for having to do the things she did, but she also realized she had no other choice; it's not like she wanted another black eye or anything.

'Good,' Adam said and looked at Sara, 'Shall we play?'

# CHAPTER 12

ANNA HEARD THREE KNOCKS ON THE DOOR, WHEN SHE OPENED her eyes and realized she fell asleep on her desk. She wiped away the tears she cried in her sleep and went for the door. As she opened it, she found a small redheaded person looking back at her, smiling. 'Hi! Remember me?' she giggled.

'Why are you HERE?' Anna wondered in her mind and stared at her, leaving poor Emma without an answer.

All of a sudden she grabbed Anna's sleeve and said, 'Let me borrow you for a minute, ok?'. Then she pulled Anna's sleeve and started running down the hall and out of the building. Anna was so shocked by the sudden kidnap she couldn't say a word or try to escape.

Emma led her to the cafeteria. The rest of the group was already sitting around a table when the two got there. 'You have to see this,' Emma said, pounting, and pointed towards them. It was only now that Anna noticed they all looked together on the same phone and appeared to be watching something.

Anna was still trying to catch her breath while she got closer to them, slowly. She didn't want to be around them and the anger she felt when she last saw them started to rise up. Samantha, who was holding the phone, looked up at her. When their eyes met, she pulled away the phone and put it back in her bag. The rest of the group protested, but Anna didn't seem to care. She turned around, about to leave when she heard his voice saying, 'Wait.'

She turned back to look at him. Adrian looked even better than she remembered. Those blue-grey eyes looked right through her and she couldn't even speak. A sudden feeling of calmness filled up her entire body and relaxed her. He walked up to her, pulled his phone out and searched for something. She scanned him from head to toe while he was focused on the phone. Her heart started beating when the thoughts of him came to mind. She thought about the way his jeans looked good on him, and that shirt too, and how he would look even better without them, without anything at all. She shook her head, trying to send her thoughts away.

'Here!' he said and woke her from the discussing fantasies she was having. 'Look,' he got closer to her, so they could look at the screen together. He was so close to her face, she could hear him breathing. 'Even his breath is relaxing,' she thought. She caught herself spacing out and ordered herself to focus on the screen.

It took her two seconds to realize what she was watching. The house they all met in, only two nights ago, was now on the screen, as the main part of a news report. The reporter, a young blond in a suit, talked to the viewers and explained the story behind and about the owner of the house. He was a former businessman who was arrested on the counts of money laundering, bribing high officials, and committing tax frauds. The state took his house and everything inside it as collateral for part of the payment he owed. His wife and two kids fled the state a week before he was arrested, and the police suspect it's due to personal issues between the couple. The police found empty bottles of alcohol in different parts of the house and they suspect the accused was the one who drank them; since he was drunk when he was caught at a bar last week. Some other parts of the house were found in a mess, but they have some assumptions it was due to the heavy storm that occurred two days ago.

The reporter returned the attention back to the main studio and the rest of the news continued. Anna looked at Adrian beside her and waited for his reaction. She sensed something strange was happening and turned around. It was only now that she realized they weren't alone; the rest of the group stood behind them and apparently were watching the report right there with them. Anna jumped in her place, startled.

She was about to say something but was cut off by David. 'That's good, right?' he said and looked at the others. 'We didn't have to tell anybody and we just got off the hook!' He didn't even try to cover up his excitement.

'See??' Samantha said, all proud of herself. Her little speech back at the house about relaxing and playing games without considering anyone, was now playing in her head.

They all seemed so happy about it; all, but Anna, that is. She turned around without saying a word and started walking back to her dorm. Now, they REALLY have no reason to see each other again, and she was more than ready to go back to the quiet life she had before.

'Wait,' he said again and she stopped. It was starting to get on her nerves; the way she could hear his smile, even when she wasn't looking at his face. He ran up and stood right in front of her. 'Can you give me your number?' he asked.

She couldn't find an answer. This is exactly why she doesn't associate with other people; they keep asking her questions she just can't answer. 'Why?' she asked instead.

'Because I want to see you again,' he said it like it was obvious this was his intention. She forced him to be direct and he never had to be like that before. It made him blush a little, even though, deep down, he liked it.

Anna, on the other hand, hated how fast he answered her question. Just looking at him started to annoy her. She didn't answer; she just looked at the ground, walked past him and kept going in the direction she first came from.

Adrian was shocked at first but then he started to smile. 'Dude,'

David walked up to him, 'you just got rejected. Why are you smiling?'

But David's words didn't affect Adrian. On the contrary. 'Just wait, my friend,' he said and patted David's shoulder. 'Just wait.'

# CHAPTER 13

AFTER THAT DAY AT THE CAFETERIA, IT SEEMED LIKE ANNA'S LIFE got back to normal. She didn't see any of them around the campus nor encountered them in the dorms. Her routine of focusing on her studies instead of her social life, put her right on track and her grades went even higher. Only at night, the effects of meeting those people took place. It seemed her nightmares were getting worse and worse; when in fact, her mind was allowing her to recall the things she forced it to forget, all this time ago. She was trying to oppose her mind, and even though she didn't have the strength, she wasn't going to stop. She was stubborn like that.

Almost two weeks had passed already from that day, and it seemed like Anna had forgotten it ever happened. The whole thing, even the night at the house, seemed to her like a distant dream she once had. If only she hadn't heard Adrian's voice coming from behind her door just now. She would recognize this voice even from far away.

'How the hell does he know where I live?!' she thought and clenched her head to the door. She heard two voices but couldn't recognize the second one. They were talking about boxes and cleaning and moving. Wait, moving?!

Anna opened her door at once, only to find him standing right in front of her with David. At first, they didn't notice her at all; they kept on talking about their plans. It was only when David said he needed to make some calls that he walked past her, stopped, and returned back to her.

'Hi, Anna,' he said way-too-loud, trying to catch Adrian's attention at the same time. 'How are you?'

'What are YOU doing here?' she said while looking at Adrian, ignoring David completely.

David gave up and went back to the hall to make his calls, leaving the two of them alone together. 'Hi, to you as well,' Adrian said sarcastically.

'What do you want?' she asked aggressively, 'And why are you here?' She had no idea why, but his presence seemed to piss her off.

He walked up to her, stood way-too-close to her face, and said, 'This is how you welcome your new neighbor?' She could hear his breath and it calmed her; his presence, so close to her's, calmed her; his smile, it all calmed her. Why?

Her face turned red when his words finally sank in. 'My new what?' she asked and pushed him away.

'Your new neighbor,' he said proudly.

'You're kidding,' she looked at the ground, trying to suppress her anger.

'Not really. We'll get this mess cleaned up first, and then I'll move in here,' he pointed back to the storage room. 'I think you and I could get along just fine if we get to know each other better. What do you say? Do you want to be my friend?' he said it in such a tone, she felt like he was teasing her.

Those suppressed feelings of anger and humiliation rose again, inside her, and she was ready to scream at him. But he just smiled and she gave up. She went back inside, took her bag and turned to the hall, slamming her door behind her. 'With all due respect,' she said without looking at him, 'you and I will never be friends.' And she walked away, leaving him behind her, smiling.

# CHAPTER 14

AFTER THEY ALL WATCHED THE NEWS TOGETHER, ADRIAN SPENT the rest of his day spacing out. He attended his classes, as he did in the past three years, in the department of fine arts, but his head was someplace else. He couldn't quite understand why this girl interested him, so much that she practically moved in, in his head. She was there when he ate, when he went to the toilet, and when he stared at the board in class; she was on his mind when he showered and even when he touched himself, in bed before he went to sleep. Her body, her face, the way she reacted to him, and most of all, the way she made him feel. God knows he hasn't felt like that for a really long time; wanting to be this close to someone else was something he only felt when he was a kid.

The days went by, and it was starting to get ridiculous. He spent every awake moment wondering what she was doing, who she was, and what was she thinking right now. He circled his apartment so many times he was starting to break a sweat. It was time to do something about it, but the lack of solutions to the question of what to do drove him crazy.

'Will you sit down already?' said David, who was sitting on his bed. 'You're making me dizzy.'

'Come on, man,' Adrian kept walking while talking. 'Help me think. How am I going to find this girl?'

'Hate to break it to you, my friend,' David said, trying to sound comforting. 'But I don't think she wants you to find her. I don't think she wants you at all.' The last sentence made Adrian stop in his place and listen. 'And besides,' David added and walked up to him, 'this one is one crazy chick, if you ask me.'

Adrian gave him such a look it made him regret and take his words back. 'Sorry, man,' he shrugged and went back to sit on the bed. 'But I mean,' he kept going while sitting down. 'She was a complete zombie, more like a ghost. Then, she drank almost two full bottles and jumped on you; as you claim she did.' He gave Adrian such a look, it was clear he didn't fully believe him about what he told him happened that night. 'Then she disappeared all day, only to come down at lunch and yell at you before she took off, faster than the storm did. you have to admit she's kind of nuts.'

Adrian seemed amused by his friend's words. 'David, my friend,' he said. 'Do you remember how I WAS when you first met me?' David stopped to think for a moment and then started smiling; he got his friend's point. 'Give her a chance.' Adrian added and looked at his friend. 'She might surprise you.'

'I guess you're right,' David shrugged and got up to him again. 'But it doesn't solve the question of how are you going to see her again.'

Adrian suddenly recalled something and fought himself not to scream at his friend. 'Dude! do you remember that day we all watched the news at the cafeteria?' he grabbed David's shoulders with both his hands. 'Emma brought her there! How did Emma know where she was?'

David thought for a moment and then said, 'Lyla gave her the address, I think. She said something about her name on a student ID. Maybe… I'm not sure.'

Adrian was so happy he almost kissed his friend, but David pushed him at the last minute; saying he'd love to, but he already had a girlfriend. Adrian hugged him tightly, turned around, got his keys, and left, leaving his friend alone and confused at his apartment.

He picked up his phone while walking and called Samantha. If anyone would know anything in this world, it's her. She could replace the CIA in terms of getting information on people. She was scary-good when it came to things like that. She picked up her phone, and it was clear right away she was busy doing something else. 'No!' she yelled, 'you do the double-flip AFTER the second jump; not before! do it again!'

'Sammy, do you hear me?' he raised his voice, almost yelling himself. He was trying to talk to her while walking up to his car.

She screamed for joy when she recognized his voice. 'Adri-baby! How are you?' she turned around, making her entire team curious about her conversation, just like she intended. She turned back to them and yelled, 'Get back to practice!' and the scarred teammates did as they were told. Samantha took the phone and moved behind the benches of the gym.

'Do you have any idea where I can find Lyla?' he said, ignoring her question. It was obvious she was looking for attention, and he doesn't have time for unnecessary conversations. 'Like, where does she live, or anything?'

'Why?' she asked. 'I thought you liked that awful girl. What was her name, again?'

'Samantha, focus!' he said while getting inside his car. He thought it would be best not to mention Anna. The two of them didn't exactly get along before, and he didn't want to make it worse.

She hated when Adrian called her in her full name. He had the gift of calling her back to order just by full-naming her. Being a law student, she didn't like the feeling of being put to trial like that. 'Ok! Ok!' she yelled at the phone. Then she added, with a much calmer voice, 'I think she said she was living on the other side of campus. Just give me a second, I'll text you the address.'

'Thanks, Sammy, you're the best,' he said and hung up the phone. Samantha was happy he called her like that again, and she still smiled even though the conversation ended; but, it didn't last long. When she turned around, back to her teammates, and saw all of their mistakes, she went back to her angry self. 'What the hell are you doing?!' She yelled at them. 'Do it again, from the top!'

Adrian drove to Lyla's place. Samantha sent him the address, and by looking at it he found out Lyla lived just outside of campus like he did. Her apartment was no longer than a five minutes drive away from his place.

When he rang her doorbell, he wondered if Samantha remembered the right address. The door opened almost right away by someone else. 'I'm sorry,' he said. 'I'm looking for my friend Lyla. Do you know where I can find her?' This person made him feel conscious of himself for some reason.

The girl who opened the door turned back and yelled, 'Lyla, get your butt up here!' at the house. 'There's someone at the door for you!' Then, she went back inside, leaving the door open. Lyla walked to the door while fixing her hair in a ponytail; she had an almost auphrough-looking curly hair, and that hairstyle didn't look good on her. She was in her pajamas, even though it was only six p.m.

'What are YOU doing here?' she asked, surprised, when she got to the door. He was the last person she expected to find at her doorstep.

'Do you know where she lives?' he said. Again, no time for unnecessary conversations.

'Where WHO lives?' she asked, confused.

'Anna. Do you know where she lives?' he said. He couldn't even explain to himself why he had to be in such a hurry. Maybe it was that deep down, in his head, he feared she would disappear before he'd be able to find her. Or was it that she reminded him of something else? He couldn't say.

'Yeah, I do. But why are you looking for her? It's not like she wants you to find her...' she looked somewhat baffled by this situation. This girl did absolutely everything to show him she wasn't interested in him. Why does he keep chasing her?

'Look, Lyla. I didn't come here to explain myself to you,' he turned serious.'I just need your help. If you know how I can find her, please, just tell me.'

She smiled and crossed her arms on her chest, leaning on her doorstep. 'Fine,' she said, 'I'll give you the address on one condition.' He looked surprised by her words but didn't interrupt her speech. 'Keep your friend away from me,' she added and looked disgusted by her own thoughts. He smiled and suppressed a laugh, thinking how she must have imagined Bryan in her head.

'Don't tell him you know where I live, and don't tell him you saw me!' she took her phone out of her pocket and showed Adrian the main screen; it was full of text messages from Bryan. He was still sending them as they continued the conversation. Adrian couldn't help but grin. His friends are crazy, just like him. 'That's all thanks to dear-old-Samantha,' she pointed at the phone. 'So don't you dare tell him!'

When he managed to get back to his serious self, he said, 'Ok, I promise,' and crossed his heart. Lyla went back inside, took a piece of paper and wrote down the address. She even wrote down her room number. 'By the way,' he said when she gave him the note. 'How did YOU find out where she lives?'

'Student ID,' she said, smiling. It surprised even her how easy it was to find Anna. 'She left it on the car's floor when she picked me up that night. Emma and I went to the on-campus dorms manager and asked him for the exact room. We said it was for a paper for class and he just gave it to us.'

Adrian started laughing at himself and grabbed his forehead. 'Why didn't I think of that?' he thought. 'Well, thanks,' he said and turned to leave when she said, 'Don't forget your promise!'

'I won't,' he said, without looking back at her, and went back to his car. He drove to the on-campus dorms, parked his car on the parallel street, and went inside. He went up to the second floor and walked all the way to the end. He was about to knock on the door when he heard a sound coming from inside. He clenched his ear to the door and listened. It was definitely her voice. Maybe she was on the phone or something; since it sounded like she was talking to someone, but no one replied.

While listening to her talking, he noticed her room wasn't the last one on the floor. He saw another, half-opened door right between hers and the dead end wall. He got up, opened the door, and immediately regretted it. The smell inside was so awful he almost threw up. He looked at the storage room and an idea started to form in his mind.

# CHAPTER 15

ADRIAN WASN'T KIDDING WHEN HE SAID HE WAS GOING TO MOVE in next door. He picked up some friends; included David, Bryan, and Andre among them; and got straight to work. They wore gloves, masks, and disposable jumpsuits on; took mops, rags and brooms into their hands and stood in front of the room. They looked like they were going for a battle against the filth in that room.

Adrian was so proud he had such great friends. Once he asked them for help, they all stepped in. David was the one who made all the calls, but he made sure they all knew who they were helping for. To top that, each one of them was responsible for a different part. For example, his friend Tommy, whom his father owned a moving company, was the one who got them the moving truck.

First, they got rid of all of the broken cabinets and doors; and removed all the broken pieces of wood to the truck outside. Then, they removed all the cleaning supplies from the inside. They took all the ladders and loaded them on the truck as well. It almost took them half a day but, suddenly, they could see how big this room was. The owners of this doorms are probably stupid if they gave up an extra room for a storage room...

While Tommy drove the truck to the damping sight to dispose of all of the filth they removed, the rest spent the second part of the day cleaning up. They cleaned all the spider webs from the walls and ceiling corners and painted them. Apparently, Andre's dad owned a DIY home painting store in the city, so he was the one responsible for the paint and brushes.

After that, they opened and cleaned the window. Once they were done washing the floor, they decided to call it a day. After all, it was almost nine p.m. and they spent all day working on that room. 'I swear!' said exhausted Bryan, 'The university should pay us for all this work.'

'Shut up, stupid,' said Danny, who was responsible for the negotiation with the university. He slapped Bryan on his head and hugged his neck and shoulder with the inside of his elbow. 'You have no idea how hard it was to actually get this room. And they even agreed to let him pay less on his rent. We should be thankful, stupid.'

Bryan managed to break free from Danny's grip and rubbed the back of his neck. Danny gave him such a look, it looked like he was going to do it again, and Bryan ran to hide behind David's back. David gave Bryan a sweet look that no one saw and turned to the others, 'Come on, kids,' he said, teasing and laughing at his friends. 'It's time to get your asses back home.'

They all, one by one, said goodbye to Adrian, who shook their hands and thanked them for the hard work. 'Hey,' said Tommy, and hugged Adrian's shoulder. 'What are friends for?' They all laughed.

'Are you good getting back?' David asked and raised his car keys, like asking if Adrian was in good condition enough to drive.

'I'm good,' he nodded and they took off; leaving him to stand in front of his new room. He still has a lot of packing and unpacking to do; and to find someone to replace him on the lease for his current place, but still, he was happy they were done for the day.

It just now occurred to him that he hasn't seen her all day. It was Sunday, and no one had classes today. She left this morning before they arrived and hasn't come back yet. It got him worried.

The next day, after he finished all his classes, he rushed back to his apartment. Adrian loaded his car with packed boxes and rushed back to the dorms. He hoped that by doing everything fast enough, he'd get the chance to see her this time. But, again, she was nowhere to be found. He even knocked on her door, but her roommate said she had no idea where she was. She told him Anna disappears and reappears all the time, but it's mostly related to schoolwork. Anna was weird like that.

The rest of the week was the same. Every day he came, carrying boxes, and every day she wasn't there. In fact, until he had fully moved into the dorms, Adrian didn't get the chance to see her at all, not even once. He started to wonder if this whole thing was for nothing or not.

# CHAPTER 16

ANNA'S EYES WERE BLINDED BY THE LIGHT. THE DOOR OPENED again and HE walked in. 'Get up,' he said and waited for her to do so. 'Hurry!' he raised his voice, "I want to take a look at you.' She did as she was told. She stood up, making that STUPID BELL ringing again. It made that sound, no matter what she was doing. She kept her head down, knowing she wasn't allowed to look back at him.

'I brought you a new friend today,' he said. She didn't move an inch, so he continued. 'He is more of a dog than a cat,' he teased. 'But I'm sure you two will get along just fine.'

He put his arm around the young boy's shoulder, like he gave him a hug, and pushed him toward the ground. The boy's knees and hands made a sound as they hit the ground, and yet, he didn't make a sound at all. Anna closed her eyes when he fell and then opened them slowly to see if he was ok.

'Help him up, Kitty,' HE said in his deep tune. Now, she allowed herself to look back at him. 'Dogs are known to be brainless imbasiles,' he continued. 'So, you must help this stupid dog get up. He can't do it on his own.' She turned to the boy and offered him her hand. He took her hand and held it tight. While he was getting up, she noticed he was the same age as she was, and was nacked as well. She looked up and away. He also had a collar, but a different one like the ones dogs usually wear.

'Good, my beloved pets,' he praised them, 'Now, play for me.' He sat on the chair and waited for them to start. Anna's whole body shook as the boy approached her. She decided to look away; maybe if she won't look at him, it'd be like it isn't happening.

The boy kissed her lips, her cheek, and her neck. 'No! No!' HE scolded them, got up from the chair, and walked toward the two frightened kids. He slapped the poor boy's cheek with the back of his hand and made him fall on the ground. 'I'll show you,' HE said, grabbed Anna by the back of her neck and forced a kiss on her. He, then, pushed her head down, slowly, against his body. He stopped pushing once she was on her knees; took off his belt, opened his pants and inserted himself into her mouth.

'You see, my dumb dog,' he said, moaning, while forcibly pushing himself inside her mouth, repidenly. 'Cats like to lick things,' he moaned, then continued, 'So you have to give them what they want.'

Anna fought the instinct coming from her throat, telling her she was going to throw up. The sounds she made while choking was like music to his ears, and he picked up the pace. Until he was done and let everything fill up her mouth, she couldn't take it and threw up on the floor.

'Lick it,' he commanded her. 'Cats like milk, don't they? Lick my milk, Kitty,' he laughed like he was having the best time of his life. He grabbed the back of her neck and pushed himself into her mouth again. 'Hurry! you don't want it to spill now, don't you, Kitty?'

When everything was clean he threw her head back and she fell right next to the boy. 'Now, my dear pets.' He closed his pants, fixed his belt, and went back to sit on the chair. He sat down and crossed his arms and legs. 'Play for me,' he said.

# CHAPTER 17

ANNA WOKE UP SCREAMING. THIS TIME, SHE NOTICED, SHE PEED her bed; and all over herself. She turned her look to the side panicked, Lily was still asleep. 'This girl...' Anna thought and sighed, 'could sleep even during the apocalypse.'

While she got out of bed and changed her pajamas and sheets, Anna heard someone knocking on her door. A quick look at her phone indicated the time was 2 a.m.. 'Who could be knocking at this time of night?' she thought and went to the door.

She opened the door and immediately regretted it. Adrian was looking at her from the other side of her door, yawning and stretching his arms. And, to top that, he wasn't wearing a shirt; again. Anna stared at her floor, all red and said, 'What do YOU want?'

'I heard someone screaming,' he said, still sleepy. 'Are you ok?' he looked in behind her and saw the pile of sheets and clothes on the floor.

'I'm fine,' she said without looking at him.

'Are you sure?' he said while he lifted her head and looked right into her eyes. She felt like he could see right through her. He realized she was crying, and in the same instinct, like that night, during the storm, he pulled her to his chest and hugged her tightly.

He calmed her down, just like that, with his big warm hug. The fear, the tears, the pain; all burst out of her, at the same time, like from the inside of a volcano. She could hear his heart beating while she was crying, and for some reason, it comforted her.

It took her a few minutes to realize what she was doing; allowing herself to trust someone like that wasn't something she was used to. Moreover, it wasn't something she usually WOULD do. So, without even recognizing her own physical strength, she pushed him out and slammed the door right in his face, leaving him shocked and confused outside.

The loud sound the door made, when it slammed, made her jump and look at Lily. This girl didn't even move an inch. She just kept on sleeping like nothing had happened. Those are really good ear plugs or she is just plain deaf. Either way, Anna felt somewhat jealous of how peaceful she was when she slept.

Anna leaned against the door, sliding on it, until her legs gave up and she had to sit down. What was she thinking? What was she doing? This is so not like her. She held her head with both her hands, trying to shake away this unfamiliar feeling.

She felt like she was going insane, like the room was spinning but staying still at the same time. All of her feelings exploded again and she had no other choice but to cry. She felt angry at herself; angry and hateful. She wanted to run away, far away, to a place she would never be found. And stay there.

# CHAPTER 18

ONLY GOD KNOWS HOW THEY BOTH MANAGED TO WAKE UP ON time for class in the morning. Both of them had almost no sleep last night, and yet they both had the strength to drag themselves out of bed. From each side of the same wall, the two of them got ready, fixed their things, and they both left their rooms at the exact same time. They looked at each other for a moment, surprised. Anna was the first to break eye contact and looked away. After last night, she wasn't ready yet to be around him.

She turned around and started walking to the bathrooms at the other end of the floor. She sensed he was following her, so she walked faster, hoping she'd lose him on the way, but it didn't work. Instead, he picked up his pace and walked closely behind her. It started to annoy her, and she suddenly stopped, forcing him to stop as well.

'Why are you following me?!' she raised her voice on him.

'I'm not,' he smiled and presented her his toothbrush and paste. THAT annoyed her even more and she ran all the way to the girls' bathroom. He smiled behind her, amused.

She wasn't used to taking morning showers, but, after last night it felt necessary. She felt the water washing down her body, washing away everything. She let the water keep running while she was busy with her thoughts. The images in her mind, of the things she experienced all those years ago, floated again. HIS terrifying smile, looks and actions rose inside her, making her want to run away again.

She sat on the floor, the water still running on her from above, and started crying. She never asked for this to happen to her; nor she ever asked it to float up. She used to think, all through the last five years, that by not focusing on what she went through, she would make it as if it never happened. She was starting to realize it never actually went away.

After she was done, it felt like she was brand new again. She left the shower, got dressed and went back to her room. On her way back, she realized she hadn't seen him when he left the boys' bathroom. She wasn't sure if it made her happy or not.

She got herself to class on time, for a change, and had enough time to get her things ready. Someone sat on the chair next to her and asked her for a piece of paper. Usually, she would say 'no', forcing the other person to simply move to a different table or just ignore her right back. This time, she surprised even herself when she said, 'sure.'

She tore a full page of her notebook and handed it to them. 'thanks.' the other said and smiled. Anna was surprised by how easy it was for her to do that. The professor got in, and the class started. So, for the time being, she'll have to find a different time to focus on her thoughts.

# CHAPTER 19

ANNA THOUGHT IT WOULD BE BEST TO AVOID ADRIAN FOR A while. If he doesn't see her for enough time, he'll eventually forget about her. Now, she had another good reason to stay late at the library.

So, the next day, she got back at almost ten thirty p.m.. But, when she got to her door, she heard noises coming from his room. At first she tried to ignore them, but they seemed to be getting louder. She took back her key from the hole, went to his door and clenched her head against it. He was breathing heavily, and it sounded like it was because he had trouble breathing.

On instinct, she opened his door without knocking. Now, they were both embarrassed. She walked in and immediately shut the door behind her. She leaned on it and stared at the ground, shocked.

He put his underwear back on and covered himself with his blanket. It was the first time in a while he was this embarrassed; in spite of being mocha-colored, his face all turned red. 'Wha-why.. why are you here?' he half-asked half-yelled.

'I'm sorry,' she said without raising her look off the ground. 'I thought you were choking or something!'

'Ha?!' he got confused. 'You thought I was what?'

'I thought you were choking!' she raised her voice and her head to look back at him. She was even redder than he was. 'you were breathing weird.'

'I was breathing WEIRD?!' he repeated her words to make sure he was hearing her right. After all, that was a really dumb excuse to walk in on someone, when they are busy doing these kinds of things. And more than that, to stay there with them.

'Yes! no! I mean...' she turned around and looked at the door. She needed to fix her thoughts for a moment.

'I think you came here for a different reason,' he said, teasing. He was only joking. He never expected her to take him seriously.

She turned to him, stared at the ground again and took her shirt off. Her eyes were pitched dark like the way they were the other night. Anyone could see her mind wasn't really there. She opened her jeans and started to take them off as well, when he got off the bed and stopped her. 'You don't have to,' he said in his calm, sweet voice. 'I was only joking. I never wanted you to-' All of a sudden, she pushed him back and didn't let him complete his sentence.

'If you never wanted me, then why are you wasting my time?' she said, furious. She picked her shirt off the ground and got dressed. After she finished putting her jeans back on, she left without saying anything else.

When she got back to her room, she started crying. She closed the door behind her and sat on the floor. Thank god Lily wasn't there that night; having to explain this situation to her would be impossible. She heard him knocking on her door, above her. 'Go away!' she screamed.

'Please,' he begged, 'just let me explain.'

'Go away!' she screamed again. It seemed like he wasn't going to stop. If he keeps this up, he might wake up the entire floor.

She got up, opened the door and looked at him. 'What do you want?' she raised her voice. At first, he didn't say a word; he just wiped away her tears and gave her an encouraging smile.

'I do.. want you,' he said, eventually. He got embarrassed, looking into her eyes like that. 'But I'm not going to force you,' he waited for a second to make sure she was listening to him before he continued. 'If you really want to.. then, I.. I..' he couldn't finish. This is as far off as he ever got in his life. It was already too much.

She broke eye contact and looked away, but at the same time she pulled his shirt towards herself. He got the hint and smiled. His arms covered her body while her head rested in peace on his chest. They both knew that tomorrow morning things might go back to the way they were before. But for the time being, they both wanted to stay like that for just a little while longer.

# CHAPTER 20

Sophia jumped out of bed and turned off the alarm. It's been six months since her sister went missing, and every day she went out looking for her. She got dressed and closed the door behind her as she left her room at the end of the second floor. In the kitchen, she found 9-year-old Bruno, eating his breakfast before he had to go to school. He was playing with his cereal, not having the will to eat them, like he did every morning since his older sister, Anna, went missing.

Sophia looked at him and recalled why she was with him right now. The second her parents called her with the terrifying news, Sophia left college and came back home. There was no way she could stay there while her baby sister was, god-knows-where.

Her mom collapsed a few days ago and was now resting in her bed; And, as hard as it was for her dad, he already left for work in order to keep the warm roof above their heads. So Sophia knew she was her sister's last and only hope to ever be found.

She took her keys, kissed Bruno's head, and went out. A few blocks down the road she saw something unusual. Focussing her eyes, she recognized a friend she hadn't seen for a long time.

Across the street, just fifteen steps away, Sara got inside a red Mitsubishi, and the car drove off.

Sophia had no idea why, but she had an instinct about it; so, she started following the car. When she realized the car drove too fast for her to run after, she raised her hand and called for a taxi. A fat oddly-looking taxi driver stopped for her. 'Please,' she begged. 'Can you follow the red Mitsubishi over there?'

It was physically impossible, but Sophia swore it actually happened. The fat taxi driver pushed the gas puddle all the way down to the floor, and the taxi flew away. Somehow, he managed to keep up with the crazy driving of the Mitsubishi.

Both cars got into an industrial area. Sophia asked the taxi driver to slow down so they won't be detected. He cooperated without asking questions. When the red Mitsubishi stopped in front of a giant warehouse, both Sara and the driver got off it and went inside. Sophia had no idea who the driver was, nor did she recall ever seeing him before. She wondered what was going on here. How did he and Sara get to know each other? And how was he connected to all of this?

The giant door shut behind the two of them, leaving Sophia unable to enter. She was determined to take a look inside no matter what. 'Leave the meter running, please,' she told the taxi driver and got out of the car, leaving the door behind her open. She ran to the giant door and searched a way in. At the most left side of the door she found an eye-sized hole.

Sophia peeked through the hole and her breath left her instantly. She saw a long line of teenage kids, the same age as her sister, standing like dolls on a shelf, unable to move. They all wore school uniforms, like her sister used to, and stood still while a tall man in a blue suit walked among them. Some of their faces were bruised, and some of their uniforms were torn, revealing half-seen body parts.

The man in the blue suit picked two boys and called them upfront. Then, he turned them in front of each other and physically forced them to kiss. She couldn't hear the exact words, but she definitely heard him yelling at them. They started to take off each other's uniforms still kissing, while the man in the blue suit circled them still yelling. Was he giving them directions or something?

Sophia was scared to death. Her eyes moved like crazy, searching between the too many faces in that line. Even though she was desperate to find her sister, Sophia prayed to god that Anna wasn't there standing with those poor kids.

While the two boys, now completely nacked, were forced to touch each other's bodies, Sophia's eye caught something. Right in front of the line, she saw another man. This one was wearing a black suit, with a black tie and black shoes. He was also wearing black sunglasses even though he was indoors. He stood still most of the time Sophia was watching, but he suddenly moved toward the man in the blue suit, only to reveal another frightened teen behind him.

Sophia covered her mouth in order not to scream. She would recognize this girl even from outer space. It was definitely her! Her baby sister Anna was standing in front of the line, wearing the same school uniform she wore the day she went missing with bruised knees and black eyes. Sophia reached her back pocket but couldn't find her phone. 'shit!' she mumbled, angry at herself for forgetting it on her desk back home.

Sophia rushed back to the car. 'Do you have a phone on you?!' she screamed at the poor driver when she flew in.

'I only have this radio with me,' he said in his deep voice and handed her the radio machine he used to communicate with the other taxi drivers. His deep tone buffered her for a second, but she shook off and grabbed the radio from his hand. 'Please!' she screamed into the machine. 'If you can hear me! Please, call the police!' She started crying. 'Please! Send them to the industrial area outside the city!'

'What seems to be the problem?' a voice asked on the other end of the machine.

Sophia couldn't hold it in anymore and she burst into tears screaming, 'I just found my baby sister in a sex warehouse!'

# CHAPTER 21

ANNA WOKE UP TO THE SOUND OF HER PHONE RINGING. HER mind wasn't fully up yet and the questions started to flout in her mind on their own. Why did she recall those scenes from a third party, when she was the one who experienced them first hand? Why those scenes and not others? And why of all people, was she, Sophia?

After the police broke into the Academia, all the kids returned back to their homes. At first, coming back home seemed to Anna like a wishful dream. It took her a while to realize she was actually there and not dreaming.

Sophia, Bruno, and her parents did above and beyond to make her feel like home again. Her parents even agreed to work less shifts in order to be around her more. Every day they gave her special treatment; she got to eat her favorite food, spend more time with everybody and got all the attention she wanted.

But for Anna it was all too much; every day she was reminded why she was getting so much attention. She felt undeserved, like for the nothing she was, they were doing too much. She just wanted to forget it ever happened and go back to the way the things were before; being alone and having an insignificant life. So she acted as if she was absolutely fine until they all slowly went back to their lives.

She changed schools after a month or two, she spent at home, but still didn't want to make friends. Trusting people wasn't as easy as it used to be. She invested herself in her books, alone in her room. People are too much to handle right now.

Because she insisted on pushing her family away from her back then, now, they had zero relationships between them. Once in a while she calls home, makes sure everyone is still alive and hangs up. That was about it. So now, when her sister's name was written on the screen, Anna was buffered by the sudden call. 'What happened?' she asked, nervous, the second she picked up the phone.

'Hi baby-sis!' Sophia said, excited. She hasn't talked to her sister for over six months now.

'Don't call me that!' Anna almost yelled. Sophia's sweet voice made her sick to her stomach. 'I just asked you a question. Can you please answer first?'

'Nothing, crazy. Everyone's ok, ' said Sophia on the other end of the call. 'Your brother has a birthday coming up next month.'

'Oh,' Anna recalled, 'On the 12th.'

'Right,' Sophia confirmed, 'I just wanted to make sure you remembered.' She went silent for a moment and then added, 'Will you make it this year?'

Anna signed. 'You know I don't like big crowded parties,' she said.

'I know. But he asked for you, you know?' she sounded somewhat disappointed. 'Bruno and I really miss you, Anna. Mom and dad too.'

'Sophia, stop it!' Anna was starting to get angry.

'Why don't you come home?' she continued. 'Just for a short visit.'

'Sophia!' Anna screamed at the phone.

Sophia signed and said. 'Well, your baby brother is looking

forward, seeing you on his birthday, and we will all be happy to see you there.'

'Bye, Sophia!!' she screamed.

Just before Anna turned off the call, she heard her sister say, 'I love you, my baby sister.'

# CHAPTER 22

DAVID WAS BUSY GETTING DRESSED WHEN ADRIAN KNOCKED ON his door. It was early in the afternoon in the off-campus dorms, and he didn't expect his friend to show up in a time like this. He opened the door while Bryan was still getting dressed behind him. 'Come in, man,' he said.

'Was I interrupting something?' Adrian teased and walked in.

'Shut up!' David protested and sat on his bed.

'What's up, man?' Bryan high-fived him and hugged his shoulder.

'Why are you here?' David said. It sounded, from his tone, Adrian WAS interrupting something.

'I have something I need your help with.' Adrian decided to go straight to the point. No time for useless conversations.

'Let me guess,' David said while lying back on the bed, leaning his head on his arms and on the wall behind him. 'it's got something to do with Anna, doesn't it?'

'Wait, what?' Bryan interrupted. 'You want to tell me that your genius plan to move in next door, like a stalker, didn't work?' He was, of course, only joking, but it made Adrian somewhat angry and David started laughing.

'No, man,' Adrian did his best to sound serious. 'I think it DID work. it's just...'

'You want to ask her out.' David completed Adrian's thought. 'But you're too chicken to actually do that,' he teased. Brian found that also funny and they both laughed at him.

'Come on, guys!' Adrian almost begged, 'get serious.'

'Ok, Ok,' Bryan said and put his hand on Adrian's shoulder. 'Look, my friend,' he said in a more serious tone, 'I think you have to go straight with this girl.'

David laughed so hard he almost fell off the bed. 'Adrian, you have something you want to tell me?' Bryan didn't like that joke and he cleared his throat to make it clear.

'I MEANT' Bryan raised his voice to overcome his friend's laughter. 'Be honest with her. Tell her you're serious about this and about her.'

'Since when did YOU become such a love-guru?' David stopped laughing and said with a smile.

'Since forever, my friend.' Bryan lifted his arms behind his head and leaned on them.

Adrian drifted away with his thoughts, leaving his friends to keep teasing and making jokes on each other. He knew now what he had to do. But he also knew it wasn't going to be easy for him. The will to run away rose up in his stomach, and he could feel the fear rising up inside. He knew what it meant; it has to be now or never.

# CHAPTER 23

ADRIAN KNOCKED ON HER DOOR. AT FIRST, ANNA DIDN'T REPLY, but after he kept knocking without stopping, she had no choice but to open the door.

'What do you want?' she asked, annoyed. She had her hair in a messed up bun; she wore sweatpants and a saggy t-shirt, and yet, she looked absolutely beautiful, the kind you can't take your eyes off of.

'Hi, to you too,' he said, sarcastically .'How are you?' She wasn't amused. She just crossed her arms on her chest, impatient, waiting for him to leave. 'Actually,' his tone changed into a much more serious one, 'there's something I need to talk to you about.' THAT made her listen. She relaxed her arms and let them fall down. 'Is it ok if I'll come in?' he asked. She nodded, untrusting, and cleared his way in.

Her roommate, Lily, wasn't there. Instead, the whole room was covered with papers, books, pens, and markers. 'Do you have a test coming up?' he asked while he scanned the room, walking in.

'Is that what you wanted to talk to me about? my test?' she replied with a question. She had that habit everytime she was asked a question she had no answer to.

'Well, no. I…' he brushed his dark hair with his fingers, looking all confused and indecisive. He cleared his thoughts and got closer to her. He looked in her eyes and said, 'I think I want to go out with you.' She looked at him, shocked. 'What do you say?' he continued.

She took a step back before she said, 'You THINK you want to go out with me?' she did it on purpose asking a question instead of giving an answer.

'No, wait..' he reached his hand and touched her shoulder, 'That's not what I meant.'

She slapped his hand off her and kept going, 'So you DON'T want to go out with me?

'Stop!' he said and held both her shoulders, so she'll stand still. 'Look!' he said and looked deep into her eyes. It embarrassed him like hell to do that since he never did it before with anyone else, but he knew he had to do it, so she'll listen to what he had to say. 'I know you feel it too. Don't run away. I know you want to.'

She was shocked; he was reading her mind and speaking her thoughts out loud. It made her feel embarrassed, scared, and most of all angry. She turned around in one move, forcing his arms to leave her shoulders. They stood like that for a moment that felt like forever.

The feeling of being nothing filled up her head. She was nothing but a cat, an animal, a lowlife being. 'You don't want to date me,' she finally said, but without looking at him. Her head was turned to the ground. Her voice sounded small and gentle like it was about to break. Something bad was going on.

'Why not?' he implored her. He thought about touching her again, holding her in his arms. He wanted so much to do something. If only he could read her mind...

'I don't do well with other people,' she stared at the floor, flashes of the past flipped in her mind. 'It's best if you just give up now and leave.'

'But,' he started.

'I'm no good for you!' she screamed, 'Don't you get it?!' Then, her voice calmed and she said quietly, 'Just leave.'

'Don't say that!' he had no idea what was going on or why she would say that. Something deep inside told him to keep going, so he did. 'You're the best for me! don't you see it?'

'Go away!' she yelled. Still, all this time, she wasn't looking at him. 'You said you wouldn't force me, right? Then leave. Now!' it sounded like her voice changed like it had something sadder inside of it now. Like she was on the verge of crying.

'Fine,' he looked at the floor. 'I'll leave you alone,' he said and turned to the door. At the last second, before he reached the door, he had a sudden feeling he knew what was going on, and he got back. He walked up to her and hugged her from behind resting his cheek on hers. He felt the wetness of her tears on his cheek; now he was confirmed she really WAS crying.

'I'm sorry,' he said and her tears started rushing out, 'I'm not going anywhere. I promise.' She turned back to him and buried her head in his chest. She whined and sniffed and whined again, crying her eyes out. And they stayed like that until she had no tears left to cry anymore.

When she was done, she was too worn out to stay awake and she fell asleep on his chest. He carried her to her bed, tucked her in and touched her cheek. 'Sweet dreams,' he said and left the room empty-handed.

# CHAPTER 24

ANNA FOUND HERSELF WAKING UP IN HER BED. THE FIRST TIME, in a really long time; a time that felt like forever, she woke up from the alarm. On instinct, she wiped her cheeks and looked under the blanket, on her bed, but she had no ichi tears on them nor pise on her bed. It made her think about the reason why. But! She doesn't have the time to sit and wonder around right now; she has a class to attend to!

She rushed up and got ready, fixed her bag and books and stormed out. She ran like hell to get to the bathrooms, brush her teeth and wash her face. If felt nice for a change, not to scrub tears and snot from her face and to wash them gently. She rushed back but then slowed down, when she saw him leaving his room and locking the door behind. He raised his head up from the key hole and looked at her. He was surprised to see her, and his smile was inevitable.

She turned her head down and waited for him to pass her by. He was just about to when she said, 'Thanks for last night,' she said to the ground. He didn't say a word.

Suddenly, she felt him hugging her from behind. So warm and calming, like coming back home. 'Anytime,' he said, then let her go and left. She stood there, smiling for a moment. Then, she landed back in reality, all at once. She rushed back to her room, finished getting ready and ran like hell to get to class.

Two hours later, she was walking on her way to the library. Another professor recommended the class for a book she said they could find in there. This time, Anna had no other class afterwards, because her professor was sick. So she had enough time to walk around and search for it. When she got there, Anna felt something strange in her stomach like something wasn't exactly right. She looked around but nothing seemed out of the ordinary, so she just shrugged and walked in. First, she started looking at the programming section, but after she couldn't find anything, she walked back to the librarian's office.

While she was standing there, waiting for Martha to show up, Anna heard a familiar voice behind her. She turned back and saw Emma and Lyla, walking together and laughing, just a few feet away from her. She turned back and lowered her head, so she wouldn't be seen. But it was already too late.

'Hey!' Emma called and rushed to her. 'What are you doing here?' she sounded happy to see Anna. The feeling, of course, wasn't mutual.

Anna didn't say anything, so Lyla stepped in, 'She's probably here to borrow a book, silly.' She looked back at Anna for confirmation. But when she didn't get any, she added, 'Let's go, Emma. I think she doesn't want us around.' She could sense Anna wasn't exactly ok, but also that she didn't want them to question her about it. 'It's best to just leave her alone.' Lyla thought.

'No way!' Emma said, still happy. She didn't have the same gift Lyla had; being able to read the room. 'Anna wants us to be with her, right?' now they both looked at Anna for confirmation, but still, no reply.

Throughout all this time, Anna stared at the floor, fighting the urge to flee this scene. She hated when people asked her questions she couldn't answer. But, more than that, she hated being cornered like she was being right now. She had nothing against them being friends with each other; she just wasn't sure she wanted it for herself. Those suppressed feelings of anger and humiliation rose up inside her again, and she was ready to let them take control of her feet and take her far away from here. Right before she was about to give in and run away she heard Adrian's voice in her mind. 'Don't run away. I know you want to,' he said. Her mind must have recorded him since she heard him saying those words in the exact same tone he used the night before.

'I don't mind,' she heard herself finally say. It took everything she had inside to keep herself in the room and not give in to those thoughts.

'See?' Emma said happily and looked at Lyla.

Lyla was surprised by her reaction. Anna was acting weird again, but this time it was even weirder. She said, 'Well, I think it's time for us to go back to research,' while looking at Emma.

'But..' protested Emma, but there was no use; Lyla pulled her arm and dragged her in the direction they both came from.

'What.. what are you looking for?' Anna said; still, looking at them. This whole situation was new to her. Confronting her feelings and taking an interest in others weren't the kinds of things she was used to. Anyone could see she was making a valuable effort.

They stopped and turned back to her. Lyla saw Anna struggling and decided to help. 'We're in the same communication class,' she shared. She decided to do it slowly. Maybe it would be better for Anna and she won't react with fire like she did before. Lyla recalled her yelling at Adrian, back at the house and storming out.

'Yeah! we never knew until we met at the house and then back at the class.' Emma added, looking at Lyla and Anna, alternately. She, on the other hand, was too naive to realize what was going on.

'We have a paper to do about computers.' Lyla was still careful with her words.

'But we never knew you were studying here!' Emma raised her voice in excitement. 'Can you help us?' she added. Too bad she wasn't as careful as Lyla was because now Anna was stuck. Another question with no way to answer. It seemed to put her off even more, and she was about to explode. This is all too much for her to handle.

If only Martha hadn't joined them now, she probably would have already run away. 'I was looking for you, dear,' she turned to Anna. 'The book you asked for last time was returned last night. I have it here if you want.'

But Anna was already too far down. She mumbled, 'Thanks,' that no one heard and walked fast towards the exit leaving three confused women behind her. Once she was out of the library, she started running. She had no idea where she was going, but still she kept on running. 'Don't run away,' she kept hearing Adrian's words playing, again and again, inside her head. She started crying.

HE came to mind. In her head, HE was still haunting her, following her wherever she went. Telling her, she was nothing again, an animal, a lowlife being. She kept running aimlessly, convinced HE was right behind her until she hit something and was thrown off backward.

'Aw!' Adrian said and rubbed his chest. They both looked at each other, shocked. Anna realized what she did and turned to run again. 'Wait!' he said and grabbed her hand, 'Don't run away!'

'Stop saying that!' she yelled at him and covered her ears. 'Get out of my head!' She sat on the ground, still covering her ears. She looked like she was waiting for a bomb to set off. He could feel her reaction wasn't, what-they-call, normal. He saw some resemblance he didn't like and it made him feel uncomfortable. So, he decided to focus on her instead of himself.

He sat down with her; ignoring everybody else's curious looks around them; put his hands on hers and turned her face back to him. They looked in each other's eyes for a moment. She now realized his words were real and not in her head like before. She took her hands down, slowly, making him do the same.

'I'm sorry,' she said and turned away, blushing. She kept showing him those hideous sides of her, and she hated that. She wished she could be better, act better, so he could see something good in her. She pulled herself off the ground.

'It's ok,' he said and tried to catch her eyes while getting up as well.

'I think I want to,' she suddenly blurred out. Her eyes opened up and she got scared all of a sudden. She was still looking at the ground, getting redder and redder by the second. She was fighting the instinct, with all she had, not to run away. Adrian was confused for a second, but he didn't interrupt her speech. 'I don't know if you meant it.. if you still want to'. She continued staring at the ground. 'I'm not good at these things.'

The context landed in his mind, all at once, and he realized what she was talking about. He got so happy he couldn't hold it in; he pulled her head to his chest and covered her with his arms. 'It's ok,' he said. 'You don't have to be.'

She pushed him back almost instantly. His hug made her feel too much and she couldn't take it. 'Don't..' she looked away. 'I.. I'm not..' the words escaped her and she felt herself drifting away in fear. 'Can you.. I mean..' she kept stuttering. He didn't say a word; he just smiled and let her take her time. After all, he recognized the inability to speak due to emotional barriers. She took a deep breath and let it go, trying to get her thoughts in order. Once she was sure enough, she tried again. 'I think I need to slow down.' She closed her eyes when she spoke. She couldn't look at him.

But Adrian didn't move. 'Do you want me to take you back?' he said. He was referring to her dorm, obviously, but Anna heard something else. He wanted to know about her past. Those inhuman things she went through. She couldn't even let herself think about them, let alone tell them to someone else. What will she do?

She was too far down in her head to hear him repeat himself until he touched her shoulder and she jumped. 'Did you hear me?' he asked. 'Do you want to go back to your room?'

Hearing the question in the way he intended in the first place made her sigh. 'What a relief!' she thought. She nodded in agreement and they turned to the car. On their way, she thought about the possibility of telling him. How would he react? Will he turn around and never want to see her again? Will he leave her alone and abandoned? But she kept pushing him away all this time. But maybe after she'll tell him, he'll understand how nothing she really was, how broken and unsavable, and he'll decide he had enough.

He will definitely hate her if she told him; that was something she was sure of.

They got inside the car and drove off. It took them almost forty minutes to get from the department of fine-arts to the other side of campus. And all through this time, they haven't said a word to each other. Adrian focused on driving and Anna stared at the view outside her window. She could see herself running on the side of the road, free and careless. She turned her head back at him and it all made sense. She could feel her heart beating, telling her to trust him.

But then, all at once it crumbled down. Her head said, 'NO!', and that was it. He'll be like Sara, like Adam, like HIM. He'll use her, like THEY did, and will leave her alone. She started having flashes again. That image of the door closing on her in that room, leaving her lying on the floor in the dark, all alone, filled up her mind. Her head was so filled up. She had no room for anything else. She had trouble breathing and she felt like she was choking on that image. She felt dizzy like she could throw up at any minute now. So, when Adrian finally parked the car and looked at her, she was no longer able to speak.

'What's wrong?' he asked, trying to help. She shook her head and the tears started gushing out of her eyes. He took a deep breath and signaled with his chin, telling her to do the same. He took another one and this time she joined him with a small one of her own. By focusing on her breath, the image slowly faded away. Slowly but surely, he helped her to calm down and breathe normally again.

'Thanks,' she said, still heaving, while she held her hand against her chest.

'Don't mention it,' he smiled. Panic attacks were something he knew very well. He, too, had to learn how to handle them every time they showed up.

His smile made her wonder again, what were his motives. 'Why are you doing this?' she said while turning her face at the ground. She became closed and untrusting again.

'Doing what?' he asked, confused. He honestly had no idea

what she was referring to. He was just trying to help if that's what she meant.

'This,' she raised her head and looked through the windshield, 'Helping me. Calming me down.' She turned her head back at him at once. 'Why?' she looked mad like he was doing something wrong. He didn't say a word; he just kept on looking back at her. So, she kept going. 'Why you're so nice to me when I yell at you? Why don't you go away? Even when I scream at you. Why?' she started crying. 'Don't you get it?!' she screamed. 'I'm nothing! I'm broken!'

The feeling of being nothing filled up her head again. She was nothing but a cat, an animal, a lowlife being. She doesn't deserve this! She wanted to run away, jump out of the car, run back to her room and hide under her blanket. Sitting in the dark is all she knew and that feeling of familiarity pulled her in. Adrian was everything she never knew was possible, and that something new was terrifying for her.

The look Adrian just gave her was the only reason why she didn't do all of this. 'No, you're not!' he yelled back and held her shoulders with his hands. She wasn't used to hearing him yelling, and it made her stop and listen. 'No, you're not,' he repeated the words in a much calmer tone. 'Look, I don't know what made you act like this,' he wiped the tears from her eyes, 'And you don't have to tell me if you don't want to. But I know this for sure; for the first time in a really long time, I don't want to run away.'

Her body started shaking. 'Why?' she asked, trying to hold back the tears.

He shrugged, then smiled. 'I don't know. I just don't. I want to help you, be around you if you'll let me. Is that ok?' He waited for her reaction. She looked at the window by her side. It took her a moment to nod back in agreement. She turned her head slowly back at him. He touched her chin slowly and pulled her head up to him.

They looked at each other's eyes, slowly getting the feeling they both were getting charged by this. It was like they shared the same energy, and it was now growing between them and giving them strength. She took a deep breath and said, 'thanks for the ride.' then opened the door and looked back at him.

'Anytime,' he smiled back at her. He waited until she went inside before he switched on the car and drove off. He still has classes to attend to.

# CHAPTER 25

THE DOOR OPENED AT ONCE, AND ANNA'S EYES HAD TO GET used to the light right away. 'Get up,' HE said and pulled her arm in such a way that forced her to stand up. Once she did, he pushed her out of the room. It's been so long since she was in that hallway that she barely remembered being here. Before she got to get used to the light in the hall, she was pushed again, back into a different room.

Inside, she saw two boys and a girl; some older, some younger than her. One of them was someone she had met before. They were all nacked like she was. HE pushed her one last time. This time, it was hard enough to make her fall down. No one moved or said anything. They just stood there, staring at the ground.

'I thought you got lonely there, Kitty,' HE said to her, 'So I made sure you'll have some friends to play with. Doesn't it make you happy?' He waited for her to reply. Now it was Anna's turn to stare at the ground, without saying a word. 'Answer to your owner, Kitty!' he yelled. She closed her eyes and started making cat noises. 'Good Kitty,' he praised her and patted her head. She prayed his hand would burn like her head felt underneath it.

'You remember your dog friend here, don't you, Kitty?' he

referred to the guy who she had to 'play with' before. He forced her head to move up and down like she was nodding it. 'Good!' he said in his praising tone and went over to the other two. Anna felt relieved when he stopped touching her.

'Meet Panda and Bunny,' he put his arms around their shoulders. The boy named 'Panda' was pushed to the ground, then kicked to roll over, and finally was left lying on his back. 'Bunny here,' HE said and went his fingers through the girl's hair, 'Will teach you how to jump.' Then he looked back at her and added, 'Won't you, Bunny?' HE put his hand on the back of her neck and forced her to nod. 'Good girl, Bunny!' he praised her and pushed her on the poor boy on the ground.

Both of them seemed used to this scenario. They didn't respond nor said a word. They both looked away when she put him inside her and started jumping, up and down, on his lap. 'Higher!' HE yelled and she picked up the paste. 'Now,' he said and turned to Anna. 'Bunny has shown you what you need to do, Kitty. So, go do the same.'

Anna refused to move from her place on the ground. So HE picked her up, pulling her hair, and threw her next to Panda. She fought the urge to scream, knowing it will only make things worse. 'I know Pandas don't like licking things, but I'll make an exception this time.' Since she refused to move again, HE pulled her hair again and sat her on the poor boy's face. 'Now, jump!' he screamed. Anna started moving like the poor girl in front of her.

'Now, you,' he turned to the last boy standing. 'Dogs are known to be brainless animals, so I don't expect you to know how to play well with others. Come here.' The shaken boy barely managed to move his feet. 'Bad dog!' HE yelled and the boy rushed his steps. 'Good,' he said when the boy stood in front of him. 'Now, sit,' he said and the boy obeyed. 'Good dog!' he praised and looked at the frightened boy.

HE opened his belt, took his pants and underwear off, and forced himself into the poor boy's mouth. 'No biting!' he yelled at the boy and forced him to open his mouth wider. HE started moaning as he repeatedly shoved himself into the boy's mouth, admiring the view of the kids on the floor.

Anna closed her eyes, trying to imagine herself in a different place. But, even though she did her best not to, she could still hear him moaning. The sound echoed in her head and stayed with her, much like the sound of his shoes when he was about to enter the room, or the sound of voice when he called her 'Kitty!'.

# CHAPTER 26

ANNA WOKE UP SCREAMING. HER EYES WERE SWOLLEN AND HER cheeks ichi, her clothes were drenched in sweat, and her body was shaking. Suddenly, she felt something she never felt before; the will to be around someone.

Ever since she met Sara, and things turned out the way they did, Anna slowly started to feel like she was turning into the last person on earth. That feeling would be described as lonely, scary, hopeless, and doomed; in that order exactly. And that was just the tip of the iceberg. Because the day Anna left the Academia, she really, truly, without a doubt, believed she was unsavable, even when every part of the situation screamed otherwise.

That's why this feeling she had right now, lying in her bed, was so unfamiliar. Trusting someone wasn't something she was used to doing or more like something she won't do at all. But she found herself doing the impossible, as she left her bed, got out of her room, and knocked on his door.

She kept knocking, but he wasn't answering. Why? Where is he? What's taking him so long? All those questions and more filled up her mind. That voice, inside, kept telling her, 'I told you! You can't trust him! you can't trust anyone!' Her heart was pounding like crazy. Her breath started to drift away. Her eyes filled with tears. The voice kept telling her she was doomed to stay alone for the rest of her life. Her mind screamed, begged, 'Open the door, please…,' but she passed out before he opened the door.

She opened her eyes ten minutes later. She was lying on his bed while he was on his desk, working on something. He looked super focused and she didn't want to disturb him. Her head started aching and she held it with her hand. She must have hit her head on the ground when she fainted. She didn't realize she was making noises, so it surprised her when he turned back on his chair and looked at her.

'You're up,' he looked relieved. 'How are you feeling?' He got up and sat on the bed, beside her, looking worried, really worried.

'How are YOU feeling?' she asked, irritated, instead and then blurred out a sigh. She closed her eyes and hit her head with her hand. It's true what they say; old habits die hard.

'I guess that means you're ok…' he grinned and moved the hair off her eyes, behind her ear. she opened her eyes and blushed.

'Aaaaaa…. I, I'm aaa' she mumbled. The words escaped her.

He smiled and said, 'it's ok, Take your time,' putting his hand on hers. 'I have all the time in the world,' he was trying to comfort her.

She couldn't stop herself anymore. She leaned in and kissed his lips; pulling him closer to her. Her hands held his face gently like they feared they would break him and by that will break the spell that created him, and he'll disappear from her life. But then, he touched her hands and patted them like he was asking for more. Then, he moved his hands, touched the back of her neck, and slowly lowered his hands to her shoulders.

They stopped, clenched their foreheads together, and looked at each other up close. He closed his eyes, trying to sink in the whole experience. This kiss, this girl. Wow! So much beauty and pain all at once. He was loving it.

Anna was so shocked she had to blink multiple times just to confirm it actually happened. She was more than ready to scold herself again for making stupid mistakes when suddenly, she felt her heart beating fast. For the first time ever, she could feel herself being alive. This feeling scared her and she wanted to get up and throw it out the window. But before she could do that, he pulled her body into his arms. She could hear his heart beating so fast it made her feel so calm she didn't want to move anymore. She just wanted to stay like this for a while.

# CHAPTER 27

ADRIAN OPENED HIS EYES AND DIDN'T HAVE THE GUTS TO MOVE an inch. Anna crawled up in his arms, sleeping soundly. They must have fallen asleep like that last night after they hugged. He blinked many times to make sure he wasn't dreaming. His eyes opened widely and they scanned the room. It's ok, he's back in his room.

He moved his body slowly, careful not to wake her up. He used one hand to wipe his eyes, while the other was locked under sleeping Anna. He started pulling his arm from underneath her head when she grabbed his sleeve, still asleep, and pulled his arm to her chest. She looked like a child holding their teddy bear. So, he just gave up and rested his body next to hers. He used his free arm and moved the hair from her eyes, behind her ear. He stayed like that for a moment, staring at her asleep.

When he was ready to get up again, she opened her eyes. Her eyes opened up too wide. She immediately realized what she was doing and let go of his arm. She sat up and turned her face toward the bed. 'I'm sorry,' she said without looking at him.

He held her head and returned her gaze back at him. 'I liked when you did that,' he blushed when he said that. He wasn't used to verbalizing these kinds of things. She blushed and looked into his eyes. Somehow, this was the most honest praise she had ever gotten, so far.

The morning sun, coming from the window, had landed the both of them back to reality. 'I have a class soon,' he heard himself saying. She looked away, and in his eyes she was acting sad. So he added, 'is it ok if I'll see you again tonight?'

She looked confused by the sudden offer. 'Tonight?' she asked. 'Why?' and immediately returned to her untrusting self.

He moved the hair from her eyes again, but she refused to look at him when he did. 'Let's go on a date,' he said and was about to get up when she grabbed his sleeve and pulled him back down, on the bed.

'I never been on a date before,' she said in a voice that was so small, even dogs couldn't hear.

'That's ok,' he smiled. 'Me too.'

And before she knew it, Anna found herself sitting at a restaurant on the main street with Adrian. It was nine p.m. and the place was packed with people. A tone of sounds surrounded them as they sat to eat their dinner.

A moment ago, when the waiter came to take their order, she found herself unable to speak. But when Adrian told the waiter she will be ordering for herself, she had no choice but to push through. A part of her got mad at him for pushing her like that, and another thanked him for letting her choose on her own.

All she managed to say was, 'pasta' and 'water' and that's what she got. He, on the other hand, ordered a hamburger and beer; and joked about not being a 'light eater.' He looked so free and careless when he talked to the waiter. It made Anna wonder if this really was his first time on a date...

She knew she had to say something but had trouble starting the conversation. Her hands got sweaty and she rubbed them against her jeans. Her heart started beating and she scanned the room, looking for the exit. She had trouble breathing and she put her hand on her chest. All of a sudden she heard him say, 'Hey. I'm right here with you,' she felt something warm on her other hand. She looked down and saw his hand holding hers on the table. 'Let's start over,' he smiled. 'I'm Adrian,' he looked at her waiting.

'Anna,' she said, in the world's tiniest voice. She still wasn't completely there. Only her body was sitting in front of him. Her mind was floating around, looking for a place to land, outside.

'Nice to meet you, Anna,' he said in a praising voice, the same one he used before. 'I'm a third-year art major.'

'I... I...I'm a...' she started. He looked at her so patient. It made her want to make an effort. 'Second-year computer-science ma-major,' she finally said. This time her voice was something even humans could hear. It surprised even her.

He looked at her shocked. She was so different from what he had expected. 'This is getting interesting,' he thought. This game was a good idea. 'I'm twenty,' he continued.

'Nineteen,' she said. Slowly, she found it getting easy like playing ping-pong, only using words instead of plastic balls. It took the stress away and it felt like numbers and codes. Like something she could do.

'I like comic books and video games,' he said, anticipating. This was an answer he was waiting for her to give.

'I like numbers and computers,' she heard herself say and immediately regretted it. She was about to say something else when the waiter came to their table with the food. All the courage she had flown out the window. He wasn't disappointed from her answer. He just never expected that to be her answer. He could see her drifting away, so instead of more information he said, 'Let's eat.' She looked away and remained mute until they left the table.

They had a nice time, eating and drinking. The food was great and the place felt welcoming. Throughout the time they spent sitting there, Anna felt more and more comfortable. She still had voices in her head telling her to get up and leave, but she could hear them less and less. Instead, her mind worked hard to come up with reasons to stay. So hard that the time flew by and suddenly the food was gone and the drinks empty.

'Close your eyes,' he said. Anna looked at him super untrusting. 'Don't worry,' he said, but it only made her worry even more. She put her hand on her eyes and acted like she couldn't see. When he was certain her eyes were shut, he asked the waiter for the check. She made tiny gaps between her fingers and watched him pay the bill. Somehow, this act seemed considered to her, and she smiled.

Adrian froze in his seat. Did he imagine this? And if he was, could this dream never end? Anna was smiling with her eyes closed and looked so beautiful. He fought the urge to kiss her. But he had no idea how she would react to it if he asked.

So instead, he cleared his throat, signaling her to open her eyes. Once she did, they got up and left the restaurant. On the way to the car, he looked at her. She looked different somehow. When they sat inside he asked her if there was a place she wanted to go. She nodded her head 'no'.

'Thank you,' she said. And for the first time, she said it without looking away.

He was so shocked, he started to blush. 'What for?' he asked.

'Why not?' she asked and immediately added, 'I mean... I...'

He smiled. 'You don't have to explain,' he said.

'I know,' she looked away, her voice getting smaller. 'I want to.'

He put his arms under his head and leaned back on his chair. 'Take your time.'

She looked straight at the windshield and talked to it. 'I think I want to tell you,' her voice was still small and a little shaky.

'I'm listening,' he changed his position in such a way that, now his entire body leaned toward her, from his seat at the driver's side. He could see and feel by her tone and body language this was important. She took a deep breath and let go. It's time.

# CHAPTER 28

THE YEAR ANNA TURNED 14 WAS THE YEAR THAT CHANGED HER life. Two months after her birthday she met her sister's friend Sara. Tall, beautiful and nice, Sara. Her sister, Sophia, was in her first year of college, and from the moment they met, they became close super fast. The day Sophia brought her home, everybody, including Anna, took a liking to her.

Anna thought Sara was one of those naturally beautiful girls that needed nothing to be considered as such with her blonde hair and blue eyes. Whenever she came to visit, which was quite often, Anna was the first to run for the door. She felt that Sara was the definition of perfection and wanted to be just like her.

The first time Sara came to visit and Sophia wasn't there, nobody gave much attention. They had such a huge extended family and they were used to people stopping by at any time. Anna was so excited from the unexpected surprise that she almost fainted. She grabbed Sara's arm and rushed to her room. She sat on the floor pulling Sara to sit with her. She was blushing, flustered, and giggled, not her shy self. But she didn't care. Moreover, she liked it. Sara excited her and she wanted to be close to her.

Sara smiled and touched Anna's cheek. She felt Anna shaking

underneath her fingers and it made her laugh. 'Such a cute lough,' Anna thought. And before she knew it, Sara's lips covered hers completely. They were warm and soft, and sweet, and they pulled her close to Sara's chest. She smelled like cinnamon and vanilla.

When Sara finally pulled away, Anna's face was incredibly red. She couldn't speak at all. Sara pulled her head to her chest and covered her up. She was warm, and soft, and sweet, and Anna didn't want it to end. But it did and Sara had to go home. Before she left, she gave her a hug at the door and whispered in her ear that she will come back another time.

The next time Sara came to visit, it happened again. Sophia wasn't there again, but nobody seemed to care. This time, the kiss lasted more than a second and Sara tried to use her tongue inside of Anna's mouth. Anna didn't like it at first. They had to do it a couple of times so she'll get the hang of it. Before she left this time, Sara suggested Anna would come to visit her at her apartment on the main street. Anna was probably scared, but she never said 'no' and that was that. Sara wrote her address on Anna's arm, kissed her cheek and left.

It took about a week or so before Anna first came to Sara's place. It was probably because the first time she went to Sara's place was also the first time Anna had ever lied to her parents. Normally, every day, after school, she and her younger brother, Bruno, would cross the street to go to their grandma's house, and stay there until their mom and dad would come home after working late again. This time, she told them she did but at the same time made 9-year-old Bruno tell grandma she was doing her homework at a friend's house. When people are used to someone that never lies, they would never assume he can.

Anna's hand shook like crazy when she rang the doorbell. Luckily, it took Sara not more than a minute to answer the door. Anna didn't get a chance to see how the apartment looked from the inside at first; she was too busy keeping up with Sara's kisses. Sara held Anna's head with both her hands and led her to the bedroom, walking backwards. They sat at the bed, still making out. Anna stopped the kiss, trying to breath for a second. 'What's the rush?' she thought.

It seemed that Sara wanted more. She looked at Anna like she was a meat sandwich and Sara was starving. Her fingers slowly lifted Anna's shirt until it was completely off. Then she started kissing Anna's neck, slowly down her chest and stopped at her breast. Anna was shaking, and not the good kind like before. This time she was scared of Sara and she didn't know what was going on.

Sara suddenly stopped. 'I'm sorry,' she said and hugged Anna softly. She kissed Anna's forehead slowly and hugged her again. Maybe she had second thoughts about this? Anna had no idea. She just knew after that Sara acted as if nothing had happened and offered Anna some tea. They spend the afternoon laughing, telling stories and jokes. Sara was sure funny. She was smart and kind. Anna liked her a lot. She could almost forget what Sara had done to her before.

It became almost too easy for Anna to lie to her family about where she was. It started with once a week, then twice and so on until she went to Sara's place everyday after school. She didn't tell her friends, nor her family, nor her teachers about Sara, even though Sara never asked her not to. She probably felt that it was quite questionable herself. She just wanted Sara's attention. She never thought it would end up like this.

Every time she came to Sara's place they would 'practice'; that's how Sara called it. 'You can't keep being shy about it, Anna,' she said. So, she taught Anna everything she needed to know about kissing, and touching, and licking, and so on. To make Anna ready. 'Ready for what?' she asked. Anna was so naive back then.

'When the time will come and you'll have to know what to do.' she smiled. Anna was a sucker for Sara's smiles, so she smiled too. And that was that, no more questions.

About three months after she met Sara, Anna met Sara's 'friend' Adam. Adam was probably in the same community college as Sophia and Sara, and the first boy Anna had met outside her family. Being a Colombian - catholic girl, she was, of course, in an all-girls high school. So, meeting boys her age, let alone older ones, wasn't something she was quite used to, especially back then. But Adam seemed nice. He was funnier than Sara and sure smiled a lot. He made Sara smile, and by that he made Anna smile too.

Adam came by Sara's place a lot. It seemed as if he was always there. At first, Anna didn't mind, 'Cause she and Sara weren't doing anything. But then, Sara became impatient and she wanted to keep 'practicing' with Anna. Even though Adam was still there, and he wasn't sitting on the couch's living room or in the kitchen. No, he was sitting on the bedroom floor right in front of them.

Anna became shy. She told them she didn't want to because of Adam's presence and she asked if he could leave. Adam and Sara laughed. 'Anna, you're just too cute,' Sara said and Adam nodded. 'Adam won't do anything to you. He doesn't bite,' she added with a tune that sounded a bit sarcastic.

Sara got her way with Anna that afternoon. Or maybe she got her way with Anna's body. Either way, by the time she was done Anna became silent. Adam sat on the bed, right next to her. Anna tried to keep her naked body hidden underneath one of the pillows on the bed. 'You did well,' he said praising. And left the room.

After that, Sara acted, again, as if nothing had happened. She kept smiling and so did Anna. She felt it was wrong but she had no idea how to say it out loud. It wasn't only until the next week that Adam had come back again. This time, Sara suggested 'the kissing game'. A game similar to 'spin the bottle' in terms of rules. Only instead of 'true or dare' the person who spins the bottle and the one the bottle stops on, have to kiss. Since Anna was not allowed to drink yet, they decided to use an empty bottle of water; and since this was a democracy and two votes triumph one, they started to play

They started spinning the bottle. Sara's bottle stopped on Adam and Anna got jealous. She wanted to punch his stupid face as he put his lips on Sara's. He looked back to her while kissing Sara; his eyes were smiling as if he was trying to make her more jealous than she already was.

It came as no surprise that when Adam spun the bottle, it

stopped on Anna. She gulped in fear. Adam seemed as if he was a hungry wolf and wanted to make her as his dinner. He kissed her quite aggressively like he was trying to force this on her. He tasted like cigarettes and grease. She wanted to throw up.

The third time was Anna's. She finally got her chance to kiss Sara again and she went for it. The second the bottle stopped on Sara. She grabbed her face and put their lips together. It was more than a kiss, so intense they both fell on the floor rolling and kissing. She was sure it would make him jealous and leave, but Adam just stood up and watched them from above. But then Sara stopped the kiss and asked if he could come close to her. He sat next to Sara on the right and Anna sat on the left.

'Kiss me,' Sara said. Adam was the first to respond. He kissed Sara's neck, slowly touching her hair. Sara looked at Anna, first right into her eyes, then on her lips. She licked her lips a second before she kissed Anna's lips again. Anna just didn't realize yet that the hands she started to feel on her body weren't Sara's. First, he touched Anna's hair, then her face, down her neck, and finally he's hand stopped on her chest. She panicked. Anna opened her eyes and looked shocked at both of them. But it didn't mean much to them. They kept going like nothing had happened.

Her clothes came off quite fast. Adam and Sara's too. They were lying on the floor naked, touching, liking, kissing body parts. It was quicker than the last time she was with Sara, but it still felt like forever. When it finally stopped, Anna remained shaking on the floor. Adam got up and lit a cigarette and Sara stayed on the floor, sitting next to Anna. 'You did great,' she said and gently touched her hair.

On her way back home, Anna fought the urge to cry. She didn't quite realize what she had to cry about. She should be happy. Sara said she did great. This means that Sara liked her, that she could be close to her again. 'I did great,' she thought. 'Then, why am I crying?'

The next day it happened again. Adam was there when Sara opened the door for Anna. This time, instead of wasting time on games, they went right for it. Anna froze in her place. She couldn't understand where she was or what was happening to her. The room was spinning and it all became a big blur. And again, with the cigarette and again, with the touch on the hair and the 'You did great'.

It happened almost every single day after school until one day it didn't. That day she was walking toward Sara's building when a red Mitsubishi stopped next to her. The car window lowered down and Sara's head peeped out. 'Hop on,' she said then laughed. God! How much Anna liked the sound of her laugh.

The Mitsubishi drove like it was going on the road to hell and it was about to take anyone on her way with it. Anna sat intentionally behind the driver's seat, so she could look at Sara all the way. She wanted to ask where they were going or what was going on, but something made her freeze in her seat. They didn't talk, Adam and Sara, at all, which was quite unusual since they always talked to each other even if they didn't talk to Anna.

The car drove into an industrial area. Anna looked at the grey smoke coming from the factories near them and wondered where they were. They got off the car, all three of them, and got inside this big white hanger, the kind they use for planes or big cars. When they got inside, Anna looked around, and she saw a long, long row of kids, teenagers like her, boys and girls, in different school uniforms, mostly catholic like hers, standing there like targets for a firing squad. Sara touched her shoulder and woke her from her thoughts.

'Go stand next to them. We're about to begin.' Suddenly, Sara's smile wasn't as comforting as before. Anna's heart was racing so fast it could explode, and she had no idea how she got to stand next to one of the boys at the end of that row. A man in a black suit walked in. The echoing sound of his shoes is something that stayed with Anna for a long time. He stood in front of the row and took off his black sunglasses. And that was the first time Anna met THE DEAN.

He called this place the Academia and the men who came there, as clients, were called teachers. They got to pick whoever they wanted, as their students. Anyone but Anna that is. No one was allowed to touch her but him; unless they were given permission by him alone. Anna was considered lucky. Compared to the other kids at the warehouse she had a good position. THE DEAN's pet. He called her Kitty. That was her new name from now on. He had nicknames for all of the students, but she was his one and only pet. Or so she thought, at first.

He was always wearing black suits with black ties and black shoes. He looked more like a businessman than the dean of discipline. She had to follow him around, every day, as he made his inspections: he would enter each and every room to see himself if the students were following all of the teachers' demands. And if they weren't, they would have to be punished.

Since she got to the Academia, Anna wasn't allowed to leave. None of the kids were allowed to. They weren't allowed to call their parents or their families, nor attend their actual schools. They slept, ate, and stayed all day at the Academia, serving the teachers who came to educate them.

Anna had to see every day the other students taking lessons no one would want to take. She spent her nights trying to keep her tears away from them. They were the ones suffering, not her, and none of them cried like she did. But when the day came that she got transferred to her own room, she wished she was back with them.

That room still haunts her dreams at night. Most of her suppressed memories were made in that room. Those kinds of nightmares make her scream at night. They are the reason for all of this. That's how broken she really is. How Unsavable she is.

# CHAPTER 29

ANNA FELT RELIEVED. THIS WAS THE FIRST TIME, EVER, SHE HAD told anyone what she went through all those years ago. It felt liberating like a huge weight had lifted from her chest while she spoke the words. Tears started rushing down her eyes but it didn't stop her. She had to get all of it out. Like she opened a den and the water was gushing out; unable to stop.

It was painful to be reminded of the things she experienced. Flashes ran through her mind as she described the feelings to him trying not to reveal anything too traumatic. She didn't want to oppose him with her past and yet she felt like she had to tell him. For the first time in her life she felt what it truly meant to trust someone.

All throughout the time she spoke, Anna looked straight at the windshield. She didn't have the guts to look back at Adrian, to actually see his reaction. She wiped the tears from her eyes and took a deep breath before she turned her head towards him.

His eyes were swollen and his nose red. He'd been crying this whole time. Anna never expected THIS reaction. She figured he'd call her a freak or realize how broken she really was and decide to run away. She never expected him to cry for her.

Through his tears, occasionally sniffing, he said, 'Can I hug you?' he looked like HE needed the hug more than she did.

Anna didn't think twice before she buried her head in his chest. He covered her with his arms, still sobbing. She could hear his heart beating and it calmed her down. She wished she could stay like this for more.

The time was close to midnight when he finally started the car and drove them back to the dorms. They haven't said a word the whole drive, and not even when they climbed the stairs to the second floor. They occasionally looked at each other and smiled, but they both felt like they had talked enough for one night. Only when they got to their doors, she broke the silence and asked, 'Can I stay with you tonight?' She suddenly realized what she did and she immediately regretted it. 'Aaa.. I.. I mean..' she mumbled.

He tried his best to keep smiling all the way back here, but now, his heart beat like crazy. She just read his mind. 'I don't want to be alone tonight,' he said it like they both shared the same feeling. He looked different all of a sudden. It seemed like the things she said in the car were finally sinking in.

So it was settled. She went inside her room, changed to her pajamas and knocked on his door. She was shaking when she did that; she had no idea what would happen, and it scared her. He answered the door without his shirt on. She lowered her eyes to the ground. 'can you please put a shirt on?'

'It didn't bother you last time,' he teased. She turned her face back to her door, ready to leave. 'Ok, ok,' he left the door open, went inside and took a shirt off his bed. He wore it on his way back to Anna. 'See? Fully clothed,' he said and spread his arms to the sides like he was presenting himself on a broadway show.

His foolishness made her smile, and for the first time, in a really long time, she laughed. She had a big rolling laugh, the kind people make when they watch stand-up comedy shows. It surprised even her and she put her hands on her mouth. 'I'm sorry,' she said shyly.

He touched gently on her hands and she took them off herself. 'You should do that more,' he did his best to smile. That made her smile too. He tried his best to stop himself from pulling her into his arms, so instead he lifted the blanket and waited for her to come closer. She walked around the bed to the other side and tucked herself in. He grinned and got himself to bed as well. It's been a long night for both of them. They could use this sleep.

# CHAPTER 30

Adrian found himself struggling to breath. He woke up at once and sat up in his bed. He scanned the room and looked for things that were a constant; closet, desk, chair, bed. He took a deep breath and let go. Once he was calm enough, he looked to his side to look at Anna; she was still asleep. He felt relieved he didn't wake her up.

He got off his bed, took his phone and sat under his window. The time was close to three a.m. when he tried calling his dad, but it had no answer. Then, he tried calling David; still no answer. He took a deep breath and let go. It wasn't the time to start panicking.

He thought about calling her. He remembered the first time he called her. It was close to three years ago; back when he was the one who needed help. Natalia was a light sleeper. He could call her right now and she would answer. He was sure of it. But something wasn't right. He looked up and looked at Anna soundly asleep. He knew now that he had to tell her. But how? After what she had just told him there's no way she'll believe him. And why would she? Even he couldn't believe it himself.

He got up off the floor, left the room, and closed the door behind him. Only then, Anna woke up from her sleep. She scanned the room and looked to her side. Adrian wasn't there. The tears started falling on their own. She felt so stupid, such an idiot. How could she trust a complete stranger like that? She buried her face in the pillow, trying to make her voice mute. She didn't want him to hear her cry, if he was any close. She didn't want anyone to hear her. She wanted to disappear, and all of a sudden, she was nothing again. Unsavable.

While Anna was dealing with her inner demons, Adrian did the same. He got out of the dorms and kept walking until he reached a public park. He sat on one of the benches and stared at his phone. He finally raised enough guts and called Natalia. She answered two rings after. 'How's my favorite person doing?' she asked on the other side of the phone.

He got up and started walking around the park aimlessly. 'Doing great,' he said in the most unconvincing tone she had ever heard. And Natalia was an expert on unconvincing tones. After all, she wasn't what people would call a 'classic therapist.' She was the one to take the call, even if it's the middle of the night.

'Now say it like you mean it, dear,' she joked.

'I'm sorry,' he started. 'I mean…' He could picture her sitting in her bed, her husband by her side. She has kids and grandkids. He was bothering her again…

'I know, dear,' her words felt like a hug, even from miles away. 'Just take your time. You'll get there,' he started crying. He missed talking to Natalia. It was nice to be reminded he had someone on his corner.

They both waited on the phone, not saying a word until he slowly stopped crying. 'Now,' she was the one to break the silence. 'Why won't you try to say what you called me for?' He took a deep breath and let go. Then she added. 'And take your time.'

'I found someone. Someone new,' he said it so fast, he had trouble breathing between the words.

'That's wonderful!' she cheered. One could see her joy for that was genuine.

He sniffed his nose a couple of times before he added. 'But I don't know how to tell her.'

'Ok,' she said, stopped to think for a moment and then added, 'and why do you feel like you should tell her? Why do YOU think she should know?'

'Because we're the same,' he heard himself say. He started crying again. His legs couldn't keep up with the weight and he fell on the floor, sitting down. Natalia went silent. She knew she had no chance to get to him like that. She had to wait until he felt safe enough to pick himself up and keep talking to her. This could take the rest of the night.

# CHAPTER 31

IT WAS CLOSE TO SIX A.M. WHEN ADRIAN WALKED BACK INTO HIS room. Anna wasn't there. He realized something was wrong and he had to find her. He walked out and knocked on her door, but got no reply. He kept on knocking until her roommate Lily answered. She had no idea where Anna was, but she sure didn't care enough to go look for her. Anna disappears all the time. It's no big deal.

But Adrian couldn't take 'no' for an answer. He ran down the hall, went out of the dorms and ran to the computer science library. When he got there, all sweaty and breathless, he saw the place was still locked. Anna sat on a bench in the hall right in front of the locked door, reading a book about something computer-related.

He started walking up to her but then he heard her say, 'Go away!'. She wasn't even looking at him when she said that. She just kept on staring at her book. That stupid book!

'Let me explain,' he started.

'Don't even bother,' she cut him off.

'I need to tell you something,' he continued.

She walked up to him and stood right in front of him. 'What part of, go away, didn't you understand?!' she screamed and pushed him back.

'Listen to me!' he yelled back. 'I-'

'No!' she yelled. 'You said you're not going anywhere. YOU said you'll stay. And you were gone last night the second I looked away so, go!'

'Let me explain why. I-' he begged. This was a long night and he was ready to cry.

'I don't care!' she turned around and started going back to her bench.

'You and I are the same!' he screamed. The eco of the empty building made his words sound even more dramatic.

The words hit her body like arrows. She turned back at him and looked shocked. 'Wait, what?!' she said, confused. At least half of her anger changed to confusion. But she was still untrusting.

He walked up to her and repeated the words in a quiet tone, 'You and I are the same.' He sounded too serious to be lying.

'What do you mean?!' she screamed at him. It was starting to scare her and she wanted some answers.

'I told you, let me explain,' he said and walked past her to the bench. He sat down and looked at her, waiting for her to sit down. She looked at him, untrusting, but decided to go and sit down. Once she did, he took a deep breath and let it go. 'Where do I begin?' he thought and looked at her.

# CHAPTER 32

ADRIAN WAS SEVEN WHEN HE LOST HIS MOTHER. SHE DIED IN A car accident on her way to work. His mother was kind and thoughtful. The kind of people they say are good, really good. He had the same eyes as her, his only memory of her. His dad owned a Mexican restaurant on the main street where he grew up. After his mother's death, his dad practically moved to the restaurant and lived there. Not too busy to make a living, but too busy to raise his child. He mostly spent time on his own as a kid, so looking for new ways to get attention outside became a habit of his.

But, Adrian was a good kid. He went to school everyday and took pride at his father for working so hard and keeping their roof over their heads. He too went to a catholic school, but a coad one. When he turned fifteen, he met his Sara. Only his was a young man named Kent. A school graduate from the same high school.

Kent came to the school on the first day of school and made a speech in the name of all graduates. He was so good with his words and had so much charisma. All the kids in the crowd loved him right away, Adrian included. He thought he was cool and impressive and he wanted to be just like him. After the opening ceremony ended, some kids went to talk to Kent by the stage, but Adrian got too shy to do that. Instead, he ran out to the yard and sat on his own.

He took out his headphones and listened to a song. He couldn't recall which one it was. But before the song ended, he felt a hand on his shoulder. He looked up and it was Kent. He couldn't believe it! Kent sat right next to him! 'I saw you from the stage,' he said while sitting down next to Adrian. 'It looked like you wanted to join your friends, the ones that came to talk to me. Why didn't you?' Adrian got shy, so he didn't say anything. 'You have something you wanted to ask me?' Kent continued.

But Adrian didn't say a word back, so he gave up. Just before Kent was about to get up and leave, Adrian said, 'I think you're kinda cool,' without looking at him.

Kent grinned and said, 'Thank you.'

'I want to be just like you when I grow up,' Adrian continued. He couldn't keep his excitement down. 'I want to be cool and good with words. Just like you.'

Kent looked at him and then put his arm around Adrian's shoulders. This was too easy. 'Do you want me to teach you?'

Adrian was so excited. 'Yeah,' he jumped out of his seat. 'Can you do that?'

'Sure,' he got up. He looked at Adrian's eyes and said. 'I'll meet you after school.'

Kent waited at the gate to school when the classes were over. Adrian remembered all the kids got jealous at him for getting in the car with him. They drove to Kent's apartment, walked in and sat on the couch. Adrian never saw it coming. Kent was so nice. He offered him a soda and video games, pizza, and candy. Kids paradise. Then he asked if Adrian would like to try a beer. He was nervous, but he did it anyway. It tasted like piss in a can and he wanted to spit it out. Kent told him not to; this is a part of his new education. So Arian finished all of the can in three sips. He coughed afterwards, but when he saw Kent's proud look, he was happy he did it. Kent passed him another one, telling him to get used to the taste. He drank two more and started to feel the effect on his head, so he sat on the couch. He still drinks it today as a reminder that now, no one can convince him to do things he didn't want.

Kent sat next to him and started to touch his thigh. Adrian's head started to spin. Kent got closer and touched his face pulling him closer for a kiss. His lips were warm and his breath smelled good. He opened Adrian's pants and started touching him. Adrian wasn't sure if he liked it or not, but he couldn't resist him. He just sat there and waited for the whole thing to end. When he was finally done, Kent touched his face and kissed him again. 'Good boy,' he praised him.

Adrian was so confused when Kent drove him back home. He got inside and could barely get any sleep that night. But on the next day Kent showed up after school again, and Adrian could see how being around him gave him more attention from the other kids. So he got in the car again. When they got to the apartment, Kent acted like yesterday never happened. He gave him candy and video games and pizza. Adrian was happy again.

Every day after school Kent came to pick him up and got him cool and fun things, but it took a week or so before it happened again. This time he didn't use the beer. He just went right to it. He kissed and touched Adrian, making him do the same to him. Adrian didn't want to, but he liked the attention and he didn't want to upset Kent. After all, he still admired him, he wanted to be just like him. He started to question that feeling. After he was done, Kent praised him again. 'Good boy,' he said and touched his hair.

It lasted a few months. He wasn't sure how many. Two-three times a week, then almost every day. Until, just like Anna, he winded up at the warehouse. It was Kent who drove him there after school. When Adrian got inside the car he said, 'I have a surprise for you,' like going to the warehouse was a present.

# CHAPTER 33

'YOU'RE LYING,' SHE SAID. ANNA'S TEARS FELL ON THEIR OWN. She got angry, mad angry. How dare he?! Tell her story back to her, changing a few details and calling it his own. Using her own words against her. She didn't care he was crying. It was fake pain. She was sure of it! He's making a joke off of her!

'You're lying!' she screamed and got off of the bench. The time was almost seven-thirty, and some of the students came to the front of the library. Miss Martha, the librarian, showed up on the inside and opened the door for them.

'I think we should find somewhere else to talk,' he said quietly and looked around. She was so mad she didn't care about them. He got up and started walking, and she followed him outside, all furious.

When they were in the open air, far from the buildings, she allowed herself to scream. 'Tell me the truth!'

'This is the truth,' he kept walking while talking without looking at her.

She ran up and stood in front of him. 'Prove it.' She put both hands on his chest, preventing him from leaving.

'Do you remember father John?' he looked away. He couldn't

bear to see her reaction. He knew she did. Father John was a regular customer at the Academia. He loved wearing blue suites and had a soft spot for young boys. Adrian was his favorite; every time he came, he chose two boys, Adrian and some other unlucky kid.

Anna vaguely recalled this kid, father John yelled at him a lot, at one of those times they had to stand in line. This kid... he had... grey-blue eyes.

Anna's eyes opened up and her breath left her body. 'No!' her mind exploded, and she covered her mouth in order not to scream. She sat down and the tears fell on their own. He looked up and away; he didn't want her to see he was crying too. It took every piece of strength left in his body to sit next to her and hold her in his arms. It was her turn now to cry for him.

# CHAPTER 34

ADRIAN REMEMBERED THE DAY THE POLICE CAME TO THE Academia, all too well. They broke inside and coughed anyone older than eighteen. Those people were sent to a life in jail and will never see the light of day ever again, or that's what the news said a few weeks after. The cops made sure to take as many photos as they could for evidence, and this was one of the most notorious cases this country had ever seen. It was on the news for months!

One or two cops gathered the kids and drove them to the hospital. They had so many kids to take care of. They hadn't had the time to ask each one of them how they felt. And the hospital staff was no different. They gave each kid, boy or girl, a quick check-up and that was it. What's needed to be was treated and that's all. Thank god Adrian was lucky; nothing but bruises and marks. No STDs, no things broken. He was sent right back to his dad. No check-ups, no therapy.

Anna was the same; lucky. Nothing but bruises and marks. No STDs, no pregnancy. Just a small infection in her vaguina; nothing that some antibiotics couldn't take care of. But also, No check-ups, no therapy. They knew some of the others got pregnant or developed desises. In physical terms, they were both very lucky, more than most, but in the emotional turmoil, they were all kinds of messed up.

Adrian couldn't go back to his old school after what happened. His father kept working long hours at the restaurant, making it seem like he had no time for his kid. So Adrian had no choice but to find himself wandering around in the streets, all day, every day. He slept with whoever, drank whatever and smoked whatever. It got him the attention he wanted. He became a master in concurring people's attention and making them come to his bed, no matter what kind, no matter the age.

He used them robotely and then never saw them again. It took him a long time to realize he was doing to them what father John and the other teachers did to him. He remembered that moment all too well, not his finest one. He was in the middle of sleeping with this girl; he had no idea what her name was; when suddenly David's voice came to his mind. Back then, he hated those words, they messed up his mind, but today he was so thankful he had a friend like him to tell him that.

He met David on the street one day. David remembered him from school, but Adrian couldn't recognize him at all. Only when David mentioned Kent to him, and how he used to pick him up everyday, Adrian was sure they went to the same school. At first, Adrian did everything to push him away, but David never gave up. They got talking and David became his confidant. He was always on his side. He said, 'You should get some help,' one day, but Adrian refused to listen. Now, in the middle of 'business', David's word's couldn't leave him alone.

David gave him a note; A friend of his father's worked as a licensed therapist, and he thought he could help. He called in but got no answer. When he showed up at the office, written on the note, the old man sent him away. 'Go away, kid,' he said without looking at him.

Adrian was just about to leave empty handed, when this lady came out from one of the rooms. 'Do you need help, dear?' she asked. Her voice sounded like a hug in his ears. Natalia saw him right away and looked right into his soul like he was transparent.

She never asked him for money. She said she's doing it because she saw something in him. She taught him how to draw and how to express himself using the right words and images. She was the one who helped him get better. She gave him the tools to rebuild himself again, to create his own dreams, to give himself hope of a better life. She taught him to believe in himself.

She taught him not to blame himself anymore. It all started by his own doing, his actions and his words, but it wasn't his fault it happened to him. He was still a kid, at fifteen. How could he know any better? Adults should take responsibility for their actions, not kids. Now that he is one, an adult that is, it was time to take responsibility for his life for his own.

And he'd been doing just fine in the last three years, since then. David helped him get his high school diploma and get into college. He worked hard and got himself a car on his own. He made new friends and learned to trust people all over again. He started drawing his nightmares as part of his therapy, and before he knew it he had a whole portfolio. Now he also had a new dream; to become a cartoonist and write his very own comic book.

He was doing just great before he met Anna. Before everything got back to him, all at once. He just needed someone at his corner again. Someone to tell him, 'It's ok' and 'Take your time. You'll get there.' Someone to take the call at the middle of the night, no matter the time.

# CHAPTER 35

THEY SAT DOWN IN THE MIDDLE OF THE STREET FOR A LONG time. The time now was closer to nine a.m., and people started walking around, passing them through. He helped her up and they walked back to the dorms quietly.

After spending last night with barely any sleep at all, they were both exhausted. The emotional journey they just experienced has tired them to the point of falling into bed, with no physical strength whatsoever. They fell asleep right away, inside of Adrian's bed, almost until nightfall.

The time was almost six p.m. when Anna opened up her eyes. She was calm and had no symptoms at all. She realized she hadn't cried nor screamed in her sleep; she had no ichi cheeks nor pee on the bed. Her clothes were completely dry. She jumped up on the floor and got happy.

Adrian woke up. 'What's wrong?' he asked, still asleep. Anna was so happy she couldn't talk. She jumped on the bed and started to dance. That verge of happiness was something she wasn't used to, but it came on its own and she couldn't stop it..

'What are you doing?' he opened his eyes and looked at her. She made him laugh, acting so crazy like that. He tickled her legs and she fell on the bed, sitting down, laughing. He liked that laugh. 'Do it more,' he said.

She jumped on him, right into his arms. 'Thank you,' she said and laughed.

'Anytime,' he said and wrapped her body with his arms full of smiles.

# CHAPTER 36

THE AFTERNOON SUN FELT WARM ON ANNA'S FACE AS SHE LEFT the computer-science building. The whole day it was too hot to be outside, but now it was safe enough to leave the air-conditioning. The days between the winter and the spring are always like that, too fickle to keep up with. She looked at the time on her phone and hastened her pace.

A week has passed since that night with Adrian, and Anna was getting better every day. Smiling more, laughing more, she found something calming and safe in him, and she had no reason to be mad at him anymore. He was teaching her new ways every day to open up and trust the world. Things he had learned from his talks with Natalia. Anna had heard so much about her this past week she actually considered going and see her herself. But it was way too soon for that, and she couldn't tell Adrian about it.

She still had nightmares, but they were coming less and less. And Adrian was there every night, holding her tightly until she went back to sleep. They practically moved in together, sleeping together in the same bed every night, and waking up together every day. This was new but also exiting, and Anna felt blessed for that.

Anna rushed to her car. She drove to the fine arts department on the other side of campus. It was a hot day and she thought about treating him to an afternoon ice cream. She was just a few minutes away from getting there; when she heard something. All of a sudden something got in front of her car and she had to break hard. She stopped the car and went outside to see if she hit something. Someone was yelling in pain, but she couldn't see who they were at first. 'Are you ok?' she asked afraid to know the answer.

'Do I look ok to you?!' she yelled and turned her head back to Anna. Anna couldn't believe this was happening again. Sara was looking back at her from underneath her car; Sara in a cheerleader uniform and a different voice. She took a step back and put her hand on her chest.

It took Samantha a few seconds to recall why this girl looked familiar to her. She vaguely remembered the night with the storm; after all, it's been over a month now. She recalled the weird girl who refused to talk and looked at her strangely. The same one Adrian had been asking her about. But Samantha had no interest in those who weren't interested in her. So she got up, wiped the dust off her uniform, and tried to stand up. She found a bleeding spot on her knee and groaned.

Anna looked at the poor girl struggling and fought the urge to run away and leave her there. Adrian's words came to mind again. 'Don't run away,' they said. And she sighed and went back to her car. 'Come on,' she said and opened the passenger's door. 'I'll give you a ride.'

Samantha hated when people told her what to do; especially people she didn't like. But trying to walk back to the medical clinic and climb up the stairs to the nurse's office was impossible with her injured knee. She had no choice but to get in the car. Once they were both inside, Anna started the car again and drove off.

They sat quietly while Anna was driving. Anna was focused on the road and Samantha was busy staring outside, when they heard a phone ring. Samantha lifted her hand, looked at the screen, rolled her eyes and turned it off. She had no patience for him, not after what he did.

Anna looked at Samantha when she touched her phone; and

smiled to herself while driving. She had her own troubles while some had others. Adrian had taught her that she could never guess a person's trouble by their look alone. He also taught her not to force anyone to speak up, like he did so patiently with her. So she'll have to wait and see if Samantha would want to tell her on her own.

Samantha looked at her upset. 'What are YOU laughing at?!' she yelled. Anna's smile must have seemed to her as if she was laughing at her. This definitely wasn't Sara. She would never jump to conclusions or yell like that. Slowly, Anna could see how different they both were. Sara had shorter hair and was taller than Samantha. They both had blue eyes, but Samantha's had some brown in them. Samantha was a loud cheerleader and Sara was a more relaxed person.

'Nothing,' Anna said and bit her lip in order to stop grinning. Seeing all those differences made her happy. She wasn't really here. Sara was still locked up somewhere else, far, far away from here.

Something in the way she looked at her now made Samantha feel different. Anna had no longer looked at her in that scary look. Instead, she was smiling. But before she could say anything about it her phone rang again. This time she turned it off without checking the caller. 'Argh!' she screamed.

This time Anna couldn't resist the bait. 'What's wrong?' she asked.

'Nothing,' Samantha said, crossed her arms on her chest and looked away. She was definitely looking upset. Samantha loved the attention and waited for Anna to ask again. But Anna took Samantha's reaction as 'leave me alone'; and so she did. She looked at the road in front of her and focused on her driving.

Realizing she wasn't going to get the reaction she wanted, she added, 'He is SO annoying!', still looking away. But Anna didn't do anything; she just kept on driving. So Samantha kept talking. Apparently, David did something wrong; and it involved Bryan. Nothing too serious, thank god.

Anna started laughing. She knew it wasn't right, laughing in someone's face like that, but she just couldn't help it. 'Why are you laughing?' Samantha sounded hurt.

'I'm sorry,' she said, still laughing. She didn't sound sorry at all.

'Come on!' Samantha said and put her hand on Anna's shoulder. 'Stop laughing!'

'Sorry, sorry,' she said and slowly calmed herself down. She hadn't laughed like that for years. And it felt so good to finally do it.

'What? You think you're better than me?' Samantha sounded hurt, hurt and defensive. 'You think your life is better than mine?'

'No, no. It's not that...' Anna said trying to come up with a better way to explain herself.

'Than, what is it?!' Samantha demanded to know. She thought for a moment and the reason popped in her mind. Her tone changed when she said, 'It's Adrian, isn't it?

Anna didn't know what to say. Samantha read her like an open book. While she was complaining earlier about David, all Anna could do was to think about Adrian. Trying to imagine them in THAT scenario made her laugh so hard.

'How did you know?' she finally managed to say. They arrived at the medical clinic and she parked the car.

'It's written on your face, you know.' Samantha said it like it was obvious. Actually, Adrian had told her two days ago, when she met him at David's, back when this mess first started. She thought for a moment and added, 'I'm happy for you. Both of you,' she looked at Anna's eyes like she meant it.

'Thank you,' Anna looked down and away. She was blushing and she didn't want Samantha to notice.

But Samantha didn't mind, she kept talking anyway. 'He was a mess when I met him, you know? Back then he did whatever. I know he told you, that's why I'm talking about it.' Anna panicked for a moment when she heard Samantha's last words. Could it be that Adrian told her about her? And if he did, what did he say?

Samantha continued without noticing Anna's reactions. 'I'm happy he found someone to be happy with,' she smiled. 'But you better not hurt him!' she added in a protective tone. That made it sure Samantha didn't know and Anna calmed down.

'I won't,' Anna used all the strength she had and looked at Samantha's eyes, 'Never.'

She looked so serious it made Samantha laugh. 'Good,' she said, trying to keep her smile away and opened the door. Anna got up to help her, but Samantha stopped her, using her hand. She picked up her phone and called someone. 'I'm at the medical clinic. Get your butt up here now!' she yelled at the phone. She hung up and looked at Anna, smiling. 'I'm good.' She closed the door behind her and walked up to a bench in front of the clinic.

Anna smiled and looked at her walking away. She made some peace with that part of herself and she sort-off made a new friend. She was so happy that she lifted her eyes and looked at the sky and saw the sun was starting to set. She shook herself off and started the car, hoping he'd still be there. She put the gear on 'drive' and drove off.

# CHAPTER 37

ANNA PARKED THE CAR NEXT TO THE FINE-ARTS BUILDING AT THE same time the students started to come outside. She got out to look for him through the crowd but couldn't see anything from afar. She walked among the crowd to the entrance; when she saw him standing there and talking to two girls. They stood close to each other, too close. One of them held Adrian's arm muscle and smiled at him.

All the possible thoughts came to her mind all at once. Who are they? Why are they talking to him? Is there something going on between them? Why is she getting so upset? It's not like he was an object she owned. She got so angry, mad angry. She wanted to scream at them, 'don't touch him!'.

But all she did was to stand there with her head down. What was she thinking? That he liked her? She was nothing but a toy to him, something to play with and pass the time. And now, he finally got tired of her and went to find someone else to pass the time with. Someone better. Someone who isn't broken as she is. Someone who could take care of him, not like her, who needed his help at taking care of herself. The tears came running down on their own as she realized the ugly truth. It was inevitable from the start. She just wasn't the right one for him.

Just as she was about to turn around and leave, she heard the last part of their conversation. 'I'm sorry,' he said to the girls. 'I'm seeing someone right now,' Anna lifted her head and listened. Her tears still lingered from her eyes.

'Come on, Adrian,' said one of them, amused. 'You? In a relationship?' she sounded so cynical the other one started laughing. She turned to a more seductive tone and said, 'That is SO not like you,' while rubbing her hand against his arm muscle.

But Adrian wasn't buying her fake attitude. 'It's true,' he said and threw her hand off of him. 'I have a girlfriend now. Her name is -' and just as he was about to say her name, he saw her standing in front of them, just a few steps away. 'Anna!' he said all happy and ran up to her, leaving the other two alone behind.

'How are you?' he said, full of smiles. 'I really missed you today,' he blushed and went his fingers through his hair. Anna didn't say a word. She just looked at him with teary eyes and smiled. 'What's wrong?' he said in a calmer tone and touched her cheek. She shook her head and started laughing. He looked at her confused.

She grabbed his arm and pulled him back to the car. Once they were both inside, she started it and drove off. She didn't say a word to him all through the drive. When they got back to the dorms, it was already dark outside but none of them paid attention to it. She pulled his arm's sleeve up the stairs to the second floor and all the way back to the room. She went through his pocket and took his keys out. It surprised him and made him jump around as she moved her fingers inside his pants. She opened the door and pulled him inside. She pushed him back to her, and now they were both standing against the door, kissing.

He stopped for a moment and looked into her eyes. 'Why?' he asked. She looked at him, confused, so he added, 'I mean.. Why are you doing this?' afraid to listen to her answer. He got scared she was forcing herself again like she did before when they met.

She held his face with both her hands and looked into his eyes.

Her face turned red. 'You said you're not going to force me,' she waited for his response. He nodded, still listening. 'And that if I really want to... then...' she couldn't finish. He pulled her face back to his and kissed her.

Anna's whole body was shaking when Adrian's hands went under her shirt. She could feel his fingers against her skin, and it made her feel shy. He stopped the kiss and looked at her for consent while he pulled her shirt over her head. She didn't say anything but she also didn't object. 'Tell me if you feel weird or bad or anything...' he said and his face turned red. He wasn't used to these kinds of things. 'And if it feels good or if you like it... then, too,' he said and looked away. Who knew looking for consent with your lover would be something this hard?

She nodded and said, 'I'll try...' in the world's tiniest voice. Her arms moved on their own and covered her chest. She was so embarrassed, self-conscious and insecure, but she was determined to overcome it. She leaned in and held his shirt slowly pulling it up and helping him take it off. She took his hands shaking and put them on her zipper. He opened her pants and pulled them down.

After he bent his knees and helped her take off her pants, he started kissing her legs. It made her shaky, excited and self-conscious. She heard herself making sounds again and immediately covered her mouth. He got up and touched her hand, the one she placed on her mouth.

'You don't have to do that anymore,' he said and gently took her hand off. 'I don't mind if you feel like or you want to be loud,' he looked straight into her eyes. 'I like your voice. You can be as loud as you want. As long as it feels good... if it doesn't, let me know, ok?' he went his fingers through her hair. He waited for her to nod or agree or something. She moved her head slowly, up and down. 'I'll do my best to tell you too,' he added and turned even redder than before.

Anna started to hear her heart beating. At first, she only felt it beating inside her chest, but now it was everything she could hear. His words went inside her ears and into her body, under her skin, and into her lungs, all reaching, filling up her heart. It charged her, gave her strength and power. She took his hand and put it on her butt. 'You can touch here too,' she said and looked away. She couldn't bear to see his reaction.

He looked at her and immediately did as he was told. He put both hands on her butt and pulled her against his body. 'Like that?' he asked and looked for her reaction. She looked away, but he could see her smiling, all embarrassed. 'Can I kiss you?' he asked. She nodded 'Yes' while still looking away. He turned her face back to him and kissed her lips while he pulled her closer and closer to him. She put her arms around his neck and shoulders and kissed him back.

She lowered her hands and put them on his zipper. He stopped and looked at her. 'Are you sure?' he asked.

Anna was starting to get angry. She pushed him back and said, 'Why do you keep asking?'. Then, she stopped and thought about it. 'It's because you don't really want to. Right?!' she walked back and covered her mouth with her hand. She was so shocked she hadn't thought about it before.

'No, no!' he said and walked toward her. 'I mean, no, I mean yes, I mean I do want to,' his words came out so wrong. He grabbed his head.

She slowly lowered her hand and looked at him. 'So why do you keep asking me?' she said, in her tiny voice.

'Because I don't want you to force yourself!' He looked at her seriously.

'Ha?' she said confused. That line made her angry. 'What do you mean force myself?! What do I need to do to be more clear?' she started raising her voice. 'Do I have to scream it out loud, so you'll understand how serious I am?!' He looked at her shocked and didn't say a word. 'Fine! I'll tell you! I want to have sex with you! ok?!'

She realized what she just said and she pushed herself back. She covered her mouth with both her hands and pressed hard. She got so embarrassed she could grab her clothes and run back to her room.

He smiled and walked up to her and slowly took her hands off her mouth, biting his lips so hard so he wouldn't laugh. 'That'll do,' he kissed her gently and covered her in his arms, slowly directing them to bed. He laid on top of her clenching his body to hers; they could feel each other's body reactions to one another, and it made them both very excited. She lowered her hands down between their bodies and placed them on his zipper. And, before he could say anything about it, she opened his pants and started pulling them down, despite the fact he was still lying on top of her and kissing her. He moved up and let her take them off.

They looked at each other and decided to take their underwear at the same time. They got up and sat on the bed. She looked away while she took off her bra, covering her breasts with her arms. They looked at each other's eyes before taking them off. They did it at the exact same time, still sitting down; then got up and turned to look at each other.

Adrian closed his eyes at first, feeling the pain in his chest raise, as he recalled the last time someone stared at his body like that. He hated that feeling, being presented like a piece of meat. He felt sick and exposed like he was put to market. He was angry, hurt, mad and wanted to break something. The tears streamed down his face as he opened his eyes and looked at Anna. 'She is probably the same,' he thought. It made him calm down and look for ways for them to overcome this feeling; together.

Anna had a flashback. She was wearing her cat collar and stood in front of THE DEAN. The tears came down her eyes and her hand touched her neck, looking for it. She could hear his voice on the other side of the door, like he'll come in any second now. She heard the sound of his steps and covered her ears. Her legs gave up, and she would have fallen if Adrian hadn't rushed to her in time. He held her in his arms, pulling her closer and closer. She covered him in her arms as well, allowing herself to fully trust him; in order to stand up.

They stayed like that, hugging naked in his room; for a while. She could hear his heart beating and it calmed her down. She raised her head and looked at him. 'Do you still want to?' she asked, all blushing.

He put his hand on the back of her neck, holding her face close and pulling her for a kiss while walking backwards and falling on the bed together. It was painful to let him in, both figuratively and metaphorically. Once he was inside of her, she could feel him in her stomach. It felt like knives were stabbing her from the inside out. She screamed and he stopped, looking at her crying. He wanted to pull out but she wouldn't let him. Instead, she pulled him deeper, using her hips. She circled his hips with her legs, placed her feet on his butt and pushed him in.

Anna screamed her lungs out. She hugged Adrian's shoulders and clenched their bodies together. The pain was strong, but she was stronger. She took deep breaths and let them go. Slowly, as they kept moving at the same pace, almost breathing together, it started to fade away. She moved her hands to the back of his head, allowing him to see her face. She was still tearing up, but now she could also smile at him.

He looked into her eyes while moving inside her and felt the pleasure run all over his body. But, he could see how much she was trying to overcome the pain and it made him want to do more for her. He started kissing her lips and moved them both backwards, so that they could sit up together. She was sitting on top of him, moving slowly. He kissed her neck and shoulders, slowly reaching her chest.

Anna started breathing heavily. This new position made her feel different. It was still painful, but it lessened and lessened by the second. She started having this feeling, like…. She was exploding from the inside out. Like tiny fireworks coming from her lower stomach and spreading to her chest and legs, going up and down at the same time. She was shaking but in a good kind of way. The kind that made her feel relaxed and calm after it ended.

He held her tightly in his arms while shaking together. He felt his heart racing faster than it ever did before. He felt that sort of feeling one never forgets having, the kind that made him feel alive.

# CHAPTER 38

THE PHONE RANG AND WOKE ANNA UP. AT FIRST, THE THOUGHT of being late to class made her stress up, but after recalling that today was Saturday, she calmed down. She questioned herself if she had the intention of going to the library today and study, but she had no memory of making such a decision. By any chance, it was time to get up and turn off the alarm.

Anna picked up the phone and was amazed to see her sister's name blinking on the screen. She got nervous something had happened to someone and picked up the call. 'Hi, baby-sis!' Sophia said from the other end.

Anna got mad. 'I told you not to call me that!' she said. Her voice was too loud and it woke Adrian up. He was about to complain about the noise when he realized she was on the phone. So instead, he decided to sit quietly and listen.

Sophia laughed from her side of the call. 'Sorry, I forgot,' she said in such a tone; it was obvious it wasn't true.

'Why are you calling me, Sophia?' Anna was short-tempered. She couldn't wait for this call to end. Adrian, on the other hand, heard Sophia's name and struggled to recall her relation to Anna.

Meanwhile, Sophia changed her tone to a more serious one.

'I'm calling about next week,' she said and waited for Anna to respond. Having not been answered, Sophia kept going. 'I'm talking about Bruno's birthday on Saturday. Are you coming or not?'

Anna got off the bed, all irritated. She had already told Sophia she wasn't coming. Why is she so pushy and relentless?! 'I already told you last month I wasn't coming. What makes you think I suddenly changed my mind?' she tried her best not to scream, but it was too late. She already raised her voice at her sister.

'His your baby brother, Anna.' Sophia tried to reason with her. After all, it wasn't Bruno's fault. His sister didn't want to be around him.

'I know he's my brother, Sophia,' she tried to calm down, but she just couldn't control herself anymore. Adrian, on the other hand, just figured out who the caller was. He sat up and paid more attention to the conversation. 'Don't try to manipulate me!' Anna's tone went higher and higher. 'I told you before I wasn't coming to the party on Saturday, and I haven't changed my mind! I won't be there!'

'Look,' Sophia said quietly. Maybe that way her sister would calm down. 'Mom and dad said they would be happy if you stayed from Friday to Sunday. But if you want to show up just to say hello it would be fine too.'

Anna opened her mouth to respond, thinking of another way to turn Sophia down when something she didn't expect happened. Adrian jumped out of bed, stole the phone from her hand, and talked to her sister. 'She'll be there,' he said and hung up the phone.

'What are you doing?!' Anna screamed at him. All the anger she still had, bottling up for her sister, lushed out on him.

'Helping you,' he said in his calm voice. He wasn't looking at her, but she was too mad to notice.

'Give me my phone back!' she walked up to him and grabbed the device back. 'What were you thinking?! Telling her that..'

'She's your family, Anna!' he raised his voice. She was starting to annoy him.

'So what, if she is?!' she screamed. 'You're only saying that because you don't have a family!'

'Exactly!' he screamed. 'I'm only saying that because I don't have a family!'

She realized what she did and went silent. 'I'm sorry,' she said in her tiny voice. But it didn't matter much now. Adrian was already furious.

'What makes you think you can push people like that?!' he screamed. 'They are your family, Anna, not strangers! and they love you! for crying out loud!' he was on a rage, but his words were right on point.

'You don't understand..' she said in that tiny voice. 'I can't tell them that...'

'I don't understand?!' he walked up to her and held both her shoulders, forcing her to look him in the eyes. 'I'm probably the only one who CAN understand you, Anna! you and I are the same.'

She turned her head down. 'You keep saying that.. don't-'

'No, you don't!' he cut her up, making her raise her head and look at him again. Then, her eyes lingered on other parts of the room. 'Don't run away!' he kept yelling. 'You look at the door like you want to storm out and run all the way down. Like you want to forget about your family, about me, about dealing with all of this. I'm telling you! don't!'

She looked at him, shocked. How did he know? How did he succeed so well at reading her mind, like that? She couldn't think; she was too shaken up from this.

So, he kept going. 'I know because you and I think the same way. I wish I could smoke this conversation away, to go into bed with you like we did last night and forget about all of this. But it will only get worse! so don't run away!'

She hugged him, holding tightly into his body. She couldn't bear looking at his face while continuing this conversation. And if she had to keep going, she'll do it on her terms. 'I don't know how to!' she said. This time she was calmer.

He started breathing deeply and letting it go, slowly calming himself down. He let her hug get to him, and all of his anger flew out the window. 'When I had to tell my dad, it was the hardest thing I ever did,' he said and touched her head. 'But I'm glad I did it. Now, my dad is the first person I call when I need help,' he went his fingers through her hair. 'Well, the second person I call,' he added and put his head on her shoulder.

# CHAPTER 39

ANNA FOUND HERSELF IN THE MIDDLE OF HER PARENTS' LIVING room, surrounded by her extended family members. She and Adrian arrived here two hours ago, after they had taken the morning train. Sophia came picking them up from the station, when they arrived. All through the drive Sophia and Adrian talked, but Anna remained quiet. Between classes and homework and papers, this week passed faster than she had imagined.

And even though she hated this whole scenario, standing here in this room was no better. At least in Sophia's car she could imagine herself running around on the side of the round; and not force-talk to people like she had to do here. She was almost at her limit, to say the least. She looked at the staircase and smiled to herself. At least the birthday boy seemed like he was having a good time. Maybe this trip wasn't a bad idea after all...

Adrian walked up to her, now. He was holding a full plate and a drink in his hands. 'What are you doing?!' she whispered to him.

'Aaaaa... blending in?' he answered, confused. 'Besides, why are you whispering? it's not like we're being watched on.' He held up his plate and ate it all. After all, he wasn't a 'light' eater. Anna opened her mouth to respond when she saw her mother's aunty walking towards her. Anna's uncle, Jose, her mother's older brother, was accompanying her.

Anna hated this part of her family; the all-too clingy side. All her mother's side of the family came here together from Colombia when her sister, Sophia, was three. They all lived together, in the same neighborhood for years. Even Sophia came back here after she finished college. Her house was just a few feet away from this place.

Her great-aunt Barbara was a very old lady by now and spoke very little English. Her nephew, Jose, often used as her translator for both ends of the conversation. Barbara said some things in Spanish and Jose translated them, but Anna didn't need Jose to translate her great-aunt's words to her; she knew them by heart. She was used to her hurtful words by now.

'Oh, isn't this our little Anna? How are you, dear?' the old lady said. 'I heard you're at college now, ha? Getting an education is not the way to get yourself a husband. After all the nonsense you did back then, seducing adults instead of holding onto your inno-cence... ahhh.. How will you get married like that? No one wants damaged goods to be their wife..'

But Adrian wasn't used to this kind of 'honest' people. He held Anna's hand all through the time those two spoke, and now that they were done, he had something to say right back. In an uncon-scious move he stood in front of Anna, separating between her and the rest. 'I don't know if you know, aunty,' he said in perfect Spanish in a perfect accent. It surprised all the parties involved in this conversation, except him.

'But there's a difference between being seductive and innocent when addressing a child,' he looked fierce. 'And kids can't always defend themselves when adults decide to take away their 'inno-cence', as you put it.. I'm sure back in the dark ages when you were young, it was ok for kids to get married at that age, and to be sold out for adults. But, need I remind you we live in a much more civi-lized time now, when these kinds of things are illegal and consid-ered as crimes?'

He sounded so fluent and coherent in his talk; Anna wasn't sure he was talking about her anymore. But, whether he was talking about her or talking about himself, he was standing there fully confident. The only thing that gave him away was how hard he squeezed Anna's hand. She could feel her hand crushing under his. Maybe he was doing it to get strength and courage from her. Either way, she was so thankful she had him there with her, this time.

Aunty Barbara said something about being insulted and turned to look away. 'How dare you to talk to my aunt that way?' Jose scolded him. 'And who are you anyway? What are you to her?'

'Her boyfriend,' Adrian said proudly. Anna was shocked. She should have been used to it by now. He had already told Sophia in the car when introducing himself as 'the guy you spoke on the phone with'; already told Bruno when they walked inside the house, and already told her parents when getting his first plate of food. He already told anyone in this room he had the chance to talk to. So, why was it, this time, that she felt his words run around inside her body? How come, this time, it made her happier than all of those times before? Why now, more than ever, SHE was the one proud to call him her boyfriend?

Barbara and Jose walked away in resentment, agreeing between each other to never talk to them again. Anna was so happy she pulled Adrian's arm back to her. He turned around and hugged her; he couldn't bear to look at her face. 'Was I being too much? Are you mad?' he asked all worried he'd upset her again. Maybe he overstepped his place too much this time.

'You were great,' she held him tightly. 'Absolutely the best.' Then they let go of the hug but kept holding each other's hands, and went to get Anna a full plate of food. The rest of the party went well; they just stuck together and faced one family member at a time. Adrian insisted they would talk to as many as they could. He was so proud to tell everyone about them, it made her laugh all through the time they spent there. Anna could almost forget why they had come here. She chose to overlook her parents' shocked looks, for the time being...

Once the party settled down and all of the guests went back to their homes, Anna's parents were free to address the new situation they had encountered; Anna brought home a boy. They weren't as conservative as the rest of the family; after all, Sophia lived with her fiance, Eddy, and they weren't married yet. But this situation was different; they couldn't let two unmarried individuals sleep in the same bed, under their rooftop. As bizarre as these circumstances were, this was something they simply couldn't do.

They sat them both on the couch and delivered them the news. Adrian was quiet the whole time her parents spoke, but Anna was on edge. She jumped up from her seat, all fired up. 'Why do YOU get to decide?!' she raised her voice. 'It's not like I live here anyway. And I didn't even want to come here tonight.' She turned to Adrian and continued her speech. 'We can go stay at a hotel or something. We don't have to-'

'It's ok,' he cut her talk and held her hand. He looked at her parents with a respectable tone. 'We'll sleep in different rooms, right?' he looked at her, smiling. She, on the other hand, was so angry at him she could explode. She could hear his voice in her head, saying, 'Deal, Anna. Don't run away from this.'

She calmed down and went back to sit on the couch. 'Right,' she said quietly. All the parties involved in this conversation were amazed by how much power he had over her; by how fast one word he said, managed to change her whole mind. They weren't aware yet of the fact it was a two-way street, and HE was worse than she was.

Now that everything was settled, Bruno walked Adrian to the second floor, and all the way to Sophia's old room. The room was the last room on the floor, on the right side, and stood in front of the only room on the left. Anna's room was the second on the left side, and Bruno's was the first; the closest one to the staircase. Bruno showed him the room and turned to leave, but before he did, he said one thing to Adrian. 'thanks.'

Adrian was left confused for a moment. What did he mean by 'Thanks'? Was he talking about celebrating his birthday? Or did he mean something else? Either way, Adrian was happy he spoke to him. Like his older sister, Bruno seemed a little closed up. He hasn't said much to anyone today, and that was his birthday party!

Even when they first walked inside the house, he was quiet. So, Adrian appreciated the gesture even more.

He turned to the bed and put his bag on the bed, thinking this room was just too pink for him. Scanning it around, he could see Pink walls, a pink desk, pink chair, and pink bed, with pink sheets and a pink blanket. He thought about throwing up when he heard a knock on the door. He left his half-open bag on the bed and went to answer it.

Anna stood in her pajamas, wearing the shyest look she ever had. She looked so good; he considered picking her up and throwing her on the bed. But he knew he had to keep his cool down and respect her and her parents. So instead, he asked her what was wrong.

'Nothing,' she answered in an unconvincing tone. Turning her look from him to the floor and vice versa, like she had something to say.

'Natalia was right,' he thought to himself, 'You can actually hear it.' He touched her hair and pulled her face up toward him, making her look right into his eyes. 'Tell me,' he said in his calm voice. It took a lot for him to stop himself and pay attention to her right now. He had to try his best not to pull her in the room with him and lock the door behind them. That pijama was just too much for him to handle.

'I don't want to sleep without you,' she said, all blushing. She moved his hand from her face and hugged him, too scared to look at his reaction. 'I don't want the nightmares to come back.'

He tried to move her and look into her eyes, but she refused to move. He had no choice but to talk to her like that, over her head. 'The nightmares are gone because of you, not me. You chased them away.'

'Not true,' she held even tighter into him. 'They're gone since you showed up.'

'They're gone because you told me,' he patted her head. She raised her head and looked at him, still holding onto him. 'YOU opened up. YOU let them go. not me.'

'Not true!' she buried her head back in his chest.

He touched her face gently and said, 'You can do this. I know you can.'

'But this room! It's too much!' she almost cried.

He didn't answer, just patted her head and waited for her to slowly let him go. Once she did, he went inside, took Sophia's pink pillow and came back. 'Here,' he said. She looked at him confused but vaguely gathered he wanted her to hold the pillow. Then he took his shirt off and took the pillow back from her hand, leaving her gasped and speechless. He dressed the pillow with the shirt and handed it back to her. 'Now, you and I can sleep together,' he said, all happy.

She got mad. Is he kidding her? Is he trying to disrespect her? 'Take it back,' she said without looking at him. 'I don't want it.'

'Why?' he asked, confused. He was so sure he solved this issue.

'Are you kidding me?!' she looked at him with tears in her eyes. He suddenly realized just HOW scared she was.

He smiled at her calmly. 'I know you can do this,' he cheered her up. 'And you don't need me for this. You're strong, Anna. More than you know,' he pointed at the pillow. 'This is just a way to show you I'll be right there with you, even when I'm not physically there.'

His words took their time to slowly ooze inside her mind. She could feel herself getting stronger by his voice alone. She allowed him to come closer and hold her shoulders. 'Thank you!' she whispered through her tears.

'Anytime,' he lowered himself so he could look into her eyes. 'Now,' he said, trying to change the conversation, 'it's time for you to go to your room now. This is already too much for me.'

She looked at him, confused. 'What do you mean?' she asked, ready to get mad again.

'You just look too good in that pijama..' he pretended not to look at her. 'It's too much.'

It made her smile and laugh a little. 'You're the one who insisted us to spend the night here. If we were at a hotel right now..' she was clearly joking. If they had gone to a hotel, nothing would have happened. But it was funny just to tease him about it.

'Don't push it,' he smiled. 'Just take the pillow and leave.' He acted as if he was mad at her.

She could see right through the joke. She kissed his cheek and said, 'Good night.'. He could feel her wet cheeks on his. Then, she turned back to her room and closed the door.

After she was gone, Adrian could breathe again. All of his air left his lungs at once and made him hold onto the door in order to keep standing. 'Damn this girl,' he thought. 'I can't with her and I can't without her,' he smiled at himself and held his head. It was definitely his time to go to sleep. He closed the door behind him and turned to bed, unaware of the fact that all this time, someone was watching him from across the hall.

# CHAPTER 40

THE MORNING CAME FASTER THAN ANNA HAD WANTED IT TO. Last night, she layed in her bed, too scared to move, until she finally fell asleep. Adrian's pillow was comforting for a while but not enough to get her all through the night. So, she woke up this morning too cranky and edgy. What a great way to start this day!

She was still lying in bed, half asleep, when she heard his door open up. She jumped up and rushed to the door. He looked at her, confused. She looked too wild compared to last night; her hair was a mess on her head, her cheeks red and her eyes puffed, with dark circles around them. 'Good morning,' he smiled. 'How was your sleep?' She wrapped her arms around him tightly, like she hasn't seen him for a long time. 'That good, ha?' he laughed and hugged her back.

Bruno just got out of his room, when he saw the two of them hugging in the hall. He covered his eyes and said, 'It's too early in the morning for these kinds of things. D on't you think?' He looked embarrassed by this.

Anna got all red and pushed Adrian back. 'I.. I'm.. sorry..' she stuttered. But it was too late for Bruno; he was already too shy about it. He turned around and ran downstairs as fast as he could, without looking back at them.

Anna looked at Adrian like it was his fault Bruno ran away from them. He, on the other hand, just laughed at it through. 'Aaaa..' he sighted. 'I wish I could be like him again. All sweet and shy like that.'

She thought about his words for a moment and said, 'Me too.' Then she kissed his cheek and rushed back to her room to change her clothes, leaving him in the hall to sigh and blush. 'I just can't with this girl,' he grabbed his head and laughed at himself.

It took her a minute or two to change her clothes and to get out of the room. She wore her usual jeans and t-shirt and socks with no shoes on. She took a deep breath and his hand as they both walked down the stairs. In the living room, she found her parents sitting on single couches; her mother was focused on the newspaper while her father was focused on his coffee. Her sister, Sophia, was there too; and sat with her fiance Eddy on a double couch. Bruno was sitting next to them, still red and shy. 'too many couples around.' he thought while wanting to run and hide.

Anna squeezed Adrian's hand and said, 'Mom.. dad..' she was looking at the ground, 'can we talk?'

The second they heard her voice, they all looked up towards her. Her mom was the first to react. She put down the newspaper and asked, 'What's wrong?'. She pushed her glasses up her nose and waited for her daughter to speak, getting more and more anxious by the second. After all, it's not like her daughter comes by this house every day; and wants to talk to them. She's usually so quiet.. And if she has something to say, it HAD to be important.

Anna's father put down his cup of coffee and looked at his daughter. For some reason, it seemed to him she was getting smaller and smaller by the second. It made him so scared he almost couldn't move. That's why he was so happy when Sophia said, instead of him, 'Can you two sit down first?' Her hand pointed toward the double couch in front of her.

Anna nodded and pulled Adrian with her on the way to the double couch. She squeezed his hand tightly so he would say something instead of her. But he didn't say a thing. As much as his hand hurt him, he knew THIS was something she needed to do on her own.

'What is it?' her mother said and sat closer, on the edge of her seat. She wanted to come and hug her child, but knew she'd push her away, like she did many times before.

Anna opened her mouth, but the words didn't come out; they refused to. She felt like she could try and scream and still, nothing will come out. She started crying. 'Where to begin?' she thought. 'And, how can I tell you?' She could feel her words, her story, will hurt them. She knew they had blamed themselves all those years, like she did to herself, for what happened to her, and she didn't want them to live it, all over again.

Adrian wrapped his arms around her and closed his eyes. He, of all people, knows what she's going through right now. He remembered what it was like for him when he told his father. Natalia was there with him and held his hand. So, now it was his turn to help someone else; and the least he can do is to give her strength.

When Anna started crying, her family looked at her shocked. Anna wasn't the one to cry, let alone, not in public like that. They knew something big was about to come out, but they had no idea how to help her. So, they all sat quietly and waited for her to calm down. But her crying just got louder and louder, like a baby crying for help. Screaming and whining, she let all of it out. Finally! She allowed herself to break in front of them.

It took her a while until she could calm down and speak. Adrian moved back and held her hand again. 'I really want to tell you now,' she said while sniffing and wiping away her tears.

'And we want to listen to you,' her mom said and the rest nodded in agreement. It was only now that Anna could see; they were all sitting at the edge of their seats, looking at her with heart-warming eyes.

# CHAPTER 41

Letting those words out of her mouth was the hardest thing Anna had done in her life. And every two sentences, she got up and tried to flee the conversation; but was stopped by Adrian's eyes and sat back down on the couch.

When she told them about Sara, they were all shocked. Sara was like a family member back then. Nobody really knew why she had disappeared for a while, back then; but now, it was clear. Sophia started crying. She apologized ten or fifteen times in a row, saying how much she hated the fact that SHE was the one who brought Sara into their home. Anna, then, picked up her courage and told Sophia she doesn't blame her for that. Sophia rushed and hugged her sister from behind, whispering, 'Thank you' in her ear. Anna's whole body shook when Sophia did that, but it was probably a good thing.

It was hard telling them she liked Sara at the beginning. She knew it would sound as if she brought that on herself. It was inevitable they would think that. After all, she used to think that way herself; before Adrian taught her otherwise. But she could take responsibility for something else she did wrong. She apologized for all the lying and the sneaking around. She was a child back then, but it was still no excuse for that. Sophia held her hand and gave her an encouraging look. 'It's ok,' she said. Then she let go and went back to her seat on the couch.

Her parents switched looks between them. Being devoted Catholics, they couldn't be ok with lying. But they also knew they shouldn't say that to Anna, now that she is finally opening up to them. It's best not to say anything at all.

Then, she told them about the apartment and Adam. How much she hated him, but she never said a thing. She told them about the warehouse; she could remember everything; the way it smelled, the way it looked, how dirty and stuffy it was and yet so big and intimidating. Then, she had to tell them about HIM.

Anna jumped up the couch and turned back to the staircase. 'I'm done,' she said. They all sensed it might have been too much for her. Maybe she just needed a break? Talking about something THIS painful.. they shouldn't push her. Even if they felt like they wanted to know more. Even though, deep down, they all knew it wasn't really enough.

But It was different for Adrian; he knew something else was going on. He could feel her closing up, shutting everything down behind her. He could feel her surrendering to those awful memories and locking away everyone else behind. He reached her hand and held it tightly, holding her back, in order not to leave. 'Don't run away!' he said, almost yelling.

She turned back and yelled at him, 'Don't tell me what to do!'. She was on the verge of crying again.

But her fake anger didn't scare him. He looked straight into her eyes and said, 'This is your chance. Tell them. You can do this.'

'I.. I can't..' she said and looked away.

'Yes, you can!' he raised his voice, making everyone in the living room on edge. 'You're stronger than you know! Tell them.' His words echoed in her mind, over and over again, telling her it was possible for her.

She bursted into tears and ran back to his arms. Between the sobbing and the whining they could hear her calling, 'I hate him! I hate what he did!' then more sniffing and sobbing, and more, 'I wish he'd die! that psycho!'. She cried and cursed and cried some more until she finally calmed down.

Her mom got up from the couch and held her breaking daughter in her arms. 'I'm so sorry, my beautiful baby,' she said in Spanish. 'I'm sorry for what those monsters did to you and most of all, I'm sorry I didn't do anything to stop it,' she started crying. 'If I had been there more. If only I could see you more...'

'No, mom..' Anna broke the hug and looked at her mother. She answered in Spanish, like she hadn't done for a really long time. 'I don't blame you for that. It's me! I didn't know how to tell you. I didn't know how to tell myself. I know you guys love me.' She looked at her family and continued. 'And I couldn't tell you. I thought you'd hate me if I-'

'We could never hate you, my life,' her father cut her, speaking Spanish while getting off of his couch. 'We had no idea what you went through. We're just happy you chose to tell us,' he walked up to them while talking. 'We thought YOU blamed US for what happened and we knew we had to be blamed for that. We are your parents,' he started crying. 'And we didn't protect you like we should have!' He walked up to them and joined the hug.

Sophia held Eddy's hand this entire time, and she now looked at him before she got up. He nodded back to her like they were agreeing on something. 'I love you, baby sis!' she said while running to her parents and sister and hugged them all together. She was crying but she didn't care. She waited a long time to hug her sister and she wasn't going to give it up over some stupid tears.

Bruno was shaking in his seat. He couldn't move an inch; he was so angry he could punch something. To think someone had done that to his sister boiled his blood. He thought about how much he loved his sister, back then. How much he wanted to make her happy, when he told all those lies, she asked him to. He thought he was helping her. So naive! He missed his sister so much in the last two years she was gone, and even more when she was home and locked herself in her room. Now, he knew the reason why, but it didn't make him feel better. He looked up at his family hugging Anna and it made him smile. 'At least, we can start all over now,' he thought. He jumped up and joined the group hug.

Adrian still stood in the middle of the room when all of this happened. He knew this wouldn't be easy for anyone involved, but he was also surprised by how well it all turned up. Anna's family was even warmer than he had imagined them to be. It took him three days to tell his dad what happened to him, back then, and he was just one person. Anna managed to tell her whole family in one day. She really was stronger than she knew.

# CHAPTER 42

ANNA CALMED DOWN AND HUGGED HER SISTER BACK. HER MOM
and dad sat by them on the couch and refused to leave until it was
already lunch time. When Anna's stomach started to make sounds,
they knew it was about time to get up. Anna's parents switched
looks between them before Anna's dad got up first. 'Bruno,' he said,
'come help me in the kitchen.'

'But,' Bruno resisted. He wanted to stay in the living room with
his sister.

'Come on,' his father said while raising his voice.

Bruno sighed in contempt. 'But it's MY birthday,' he said and
dragged himself off the couch.

Anna smiled and grabbed his hand when he walked past her.
'Make me something good,' she said.

He jumped and hugged her tightly. 'You bet,' he whispered.
Then he got up and rushed to the kitchen.

Anna's mom turned to Adrian. He sat down earlier, next to
Eddy, when the two sisters moved their hug to the couch. 'Can I
have a word with you?' she asked and got off of her seat.

'Sure,' he said and followed her lead. She walked him up stairs
to Anna's old room. He scanned the room before he walked in. For

someone else, this would look like a regular teenager's room, a bed, a closet, a table, and a chair. But in Adrian's eyes it looked completely different. He could see the scratches on the walls next to the bad, the over washed bed-sheets from pee stains, the dusty windows nobody bothered to open for years. Compared to Sophia's old room, this looked like a teenage girl's nightmare.

Anna's mother sat on her daughter's unmade bed and turned to Adrian. 'Sit,' she said and pointed next to her. Anna's mother, Lucia, was a large woman, probably in her fifties, but she looked younger. For a moment, back there in the living room, she reminded Adrian of his own mom, warm, kind, and loving. It made him miss her even more. But for now he did as he was told and sat by Lucia's side.

'You probably wonder why I called you up here,' she said with a broken accent. 'I..' she said and then regretted it. 'Is it ok if I'll speak in Spanish?' she asked in Spanish. Adrian smiled and nodded his head up and down. 'Good,' she said, relieved she could speak fluently, without worrying about the language barrier.

'You want to talk to me about Anna,' he said with a perfect accent. It made her feel surprised. She almost started a different conversation when she was about to ask him about his origin, but she stopped herself at the last minute. She'll have to do that at another time. So, for now, she just nodded in agreement.

'Yes,' she said and looked at the young man. He looked no more than twenty years old, so young in her eyes. 'Last night you..' she took a deep breath, 'you're a good kid, I can tell. Your parents raised you well. You have respect in you.'

Adrian started to blush. He wasn't expecting to be flattered like that and by his girlfriend's mother, no less.. 'How can you tell?' he asked.

'Last night, when my daughter tried to come inside your room,' she looked straight at him like she was revealing his secret. He was shocked, she saw them. But how? Last night, he was sure just the two of them were in the hall, alone. He didn't see anyone else back then, but then again, it was a dark hall.

'You told her no,' she kept talking, checking his reactions while speaking. He got scared for a moment. Maybe she didn't approve of him or his actions? He didn't want to have a bad start with his girlfriend's parents..

'I'd like to thank you for that,' she smiled. It made him blush even more.

'Thank me?' he asked, confused. 'For saying no?'

'Exactly,' she answered. 'We, as her parents, asked the two of you something that was important to us. I'm sure it didn't mean much to you, but still you respected us. It meant so much for us. Alberto also agreed with me..' She was referring to Anna's dad. 'And now, before,' she pointed at the door. 'How did you know?'

'What do you mean?' he asked.

'When she wanted to leave,' she grabbed her head, recalling the pain she felt for her daughter. 'You yelled at her.'

'I...I'm sorry about that,' he said ashamed. He wasn't paying attention to anyone else when it happened. He was too focused on Anna, and how to help her get this through. He never meant to hurt her or the rest of them.

'Don't be,' she said. 'I know as her mother I'm supposed to yell at you right now. And if this was a normal conversation, I would have. Trust me. But, for today, I'd like to give you a hug.' She opened her arms and pulled him to her chest. He got squeezed between her arms and chest, struggling to breath. But the way she hugged him, with so much love, made him surrender. 'Thank you for taking care of my baby,' she said.

'Anytime,' he smiled and hugged her back. Then they slowly let go and smiled at each other.

'So, tell me,' Lucia said in her gossiping tone. 'Where is your family from?'

Adrian smiled and was thankful for the change of conversation. 'So,' he said and started to talk about his extended family.

# CHAPTER 43

WHILE HER MOTHER WAS INTERROGATING ADRIAN ON EVERY part of his extended family, Anna was still sitting on the couch, lying in her sister's embrace. She enjoyed this new experience, as well as her sister, and they both didn't want to stop and lose it. So, it was understandable they both got upset when they heard a phone ringing on the table.

'Whose is it anyway?' Sophia said, all grumpy. She didn't like how the stupid phone ring interrupted her quiet quality time with her sister. Anna moved her and sat up, approaching the table. She didn't see her phone anywhere. Instead, she saw Adrian's.

On the screen she could see a familiar name blinking. 'David,' it said. Anna got nervous. 'What if Adrian gets mad?' she thought. 'I shouldn't touch his phone like that.' She waited a few seconds, and the phone stopped on his own. But just two seconds after it stopped, it rang again, blinking David's name again.

'Maybe something bad happened?' she thought, getting scared. 'Maybe I should just answer, make sure nothing happened..' she reached her hand and held the phone.

'Whose is it?' Sophia scared her, waking her from her thoughts. 'Do you know?' Anna decided not to share any hurtful information.

She just grabbed the phone and answered it like it was her own. She got up and went to the kitchen.

It was clear, David wasn't expecting anyone to pick up the phone when Anna answered it. It sounded like he was too busy talking to someone else. 'No, no. Just put it somewhere else. It won't fit there, trust me,' he said.

'David,' Anna said to the phone, all quietly. She looked up and saw her father and brother busy making food. It made her feel obligated to keep her voice low, so she won't interrupt them.

'Ha?' he said and stopped to look at his phone. 'Isn't this Adrian's phone number?' he said, all confused.

'It is,' Anna said, in such a small voice it was shocking that David even heard her. 'It's Anna.'

'Oh, Anna!' he sounded happy. Maybe more, because he called the right number. 'Is Adrian with you? Sorry if I'm being too much right now. I'm just looking for him for a long time.'

'Why?' she asked. She was confused but she also didn't want to nose in too much. 'I mean-' she tried to explain.

But David didn't notice that; he just kept going. 'Everybody's here. We're waiting for him. Where are you two anyway?'

'We went to visit my family for the weekend,' she heard herself say. 'Out of town. Why?' She wasn't used to herself giving out information like that. It shocked even her.

'Oh, no!' he sounded like something bad was happening to him. 'Really?' he asked, even though he knew her answer wouldn't change.

'What's wrong?' she asked and immediately regretted it. She was too nosy.

He stopped and pondered for a moment. 'Ah! You don't know, don't you?' he asked.

'Know what?' she got even more confused than before.

'Today is Adrian's birthday,' he said, all happy. Anna was so shocked she didn't say a word. 'I'll take that as you didn't,' he sighed. 'Figures.. you know, he always does that, forgetting himself. He focuses on someone else instead of his own. I don't know if he was born like that or because he was-' he stopped himself before he said something more. 'Anyway,' he decided to change the conversation. 'Tell him I called and he'll get for this. Now, I have to clean this mess up. Ok, everyone,' he was clearly talking to someone else again. 'The birthday boy is out of town. Let's get this mess cleaned up.' And he hung up the phone.

Anna slowly lowered the phone down. She looked at her father and brother, still busy making lunch. She was still scared Adrian would be mad at her for taking his phone and answering his calls. Ok, one call, but still.. But even more than that, she was too shocked he had done that. He passed on his own birthday for her brother's. For someone he barely even knew. Why?

She heard them come downstairs and rushed to the staircase. She got so fired up and wanted to ask him all those questions. But her brother got out of the kitchen the second she was able to look Adrian in the eyes. 'Food's ready,' Bruno said and went back inside to finish setting the table. And just like that her chance flew out the window, as he walked past her with her mother.

'Anna,' Sophia called from the kitchen. 'Didn't you hear? Food's ready.' And just like that everything went back to normal. She was fourteen again, and for a moment she could act as if nothing had happened.

'I'm coming!' she yelled backward and went back to the kitchen.

# CHAPTER 44

ANNA SAT INSIDE THE TRAIN AND LOOKED AT ADRIAN ASLEEP. IT was about 3 a.m. when she turned her look from the view outside back at him. They got on this train just an hour ago and they still had another one to go. Sophia drove them back to the train station; and said goodbye a thousand times before she drove back home. It made Anna feel embarrassed but also lucky; her sister was just something else.

Adrian yawned and fell asleep the second he sat down, and Anna planned to do so as well. She was so exhausted and tired from the day she had, and the lack of sleep from last night wasn't much help. But for some reason she just couldn't. Her mind was full of questions, full of wonderings; all needed clarifications. She watched him, thinking he looked so peaceful in his sleep; and wished she could do the same.

She had something bothering her mind for days now, and it was time to tell him. The decision of what to say was starting to form in her head as he moved his head from side to side, ready to wake up. He opened his eyes and looked at her. At first, he was a little nervous to find out she was looking at him in his sleep. His smile came later as he felt the joy of having her as the first thing he looked at when he woke up. He rubbed his eyes and sat up straight.

She leaned her arm on the window and her head on her hand as she looked at him. Her smile wasn't her usual one; and felt more like an obligatory one than a real one. 'What's wrong?' he asked, in the voice of someone who just woke up. He cleared his throat and cleaned his eyes with his fingers. She moved slowly as she opened her backpack, took out a bottle of water and handed it to him. 'Thanks,' he said and drank the water.

She went back to her position on the window. Her looks were definitely telling him something. He took another sip and swallowed it; when he suddenly realized questions weren't the way to do this. 'Tell me,' he said and closed the bottle.

'Can I ask you something?' she asked. Her voice was soft and she seemed relaxed, definitely not her usual self. It got him worried and he moved to the edge of his seat. He wasn't sure what to say, so he just nodded his head up and down, untrusting.

She closed her eyes, took a deep breath and let it go before she reopened them. 'How did it feel the first time you met Natalia?' He looked at her confused. She wanted to explain herself better, but the better words just didn't come. So she simply said, 'I think I need help,' in a calm face, and lowered her eyes to the ground.

His eyes opened up, and he looked at her, shocked. He didn't expect this. A wave of happiness flooded him as the news finally sinked in. He tried his best not to jump to her seat and hug her. It's not the time for that. Instead, he cleared his throat and tried to look more serious. 'I'm listening.' he said.

'When you told me about her,' she looked away, towards the window. 'It sounded like she really helped you.' She found herself unable to look at him directly when she said the words. 'You keep telling me she taught you this and taught you that. So, I thought maybe she.. she could..' she sighed and buried her head in her hands.

She knew exactly what's going on in his head right now. He won't say a thing to her until she is finished. She could feel his smile on her even though she wasn't looking at him. They both knew what she had to say next, and this conversation won't end until she will say it. She lifted her head slowly and looked back at him. She was right. She smiled back; this time it was a genuine one. Her eyes filled up with tears as she said the words, 'I think she can help me too. Can you please give me the number?'

Now it was the right time to do what he wanted to do all along. He got up from his seat and moved next to her, covering her in his arms. She leaned on his chest and hugged him back. He kissed her head and then held her chin up, looking into her eyes. 'Just tell me when,' he said, smiling. Her tears kept falling even though she was smiling now. She leaned in and kissed him. He kissed her back, holding her tightly in his arms.

They will have kept going like that for hours if the conductor hasn't shown up now. He cleared his throat and waited for them to notice him. Adrian and Anna slowly turned back to look at him, embarrassed and ashamed. 'This is a public train,' he said in a serious tone, like he was scolding them.

Adrian fought the instinct to laugh as he said, 'We're deeply sorry, sir. It won't happen again.' He looked at Anna, who was too embarrassed to look at the conductor; she only nodded her head in agreement. The conductor looked at them with an untrusting look, probably for a warning, and turned to walk away. The second he was far enough, Adrian allowed himself to laugh.

Anna looked at him, confused. 'Oh, come on!' he said, trying to keep his voice down, in case the conductor comes back again. 'This is hilarious!' She got why he was laughing; that wasn't the reason for her confusion. It was due to the fact this was the first time she heard him laughing like that. She wondered why. But his laugh was big and contagious; she just couldn't ignore it. She started laughing as well. They looked at each other, laughing away, until they were able to calm down.

He touched her hair on her head and looked at her, trying to suppress his laugh. She tried to do the same when she suddenly recalled something. She stopped and focused on her thoughts for a moment; then, she went quiet as she recalled about when David told her about Adrian's birthday. Her face turned serious. If that's true, then she was a terrible girlfriend. How could she not know?

He could see her drifting away and he had no idea why. So he said, 'Tell me what's wrong.' in the hope that she will.

She looked down and said, 'Happy birthday.' It shook him off. He forgot all about that, completely. He didn't even remember telling her. How did she know? He was about to ask her that when she added, 'David called when you were talking to my mom.' She couldn't look at him, fearing he'll get mad, she touched his phone with no permission. But he still hasn't said a thing so she thought it would be safe enough to continue. 'He was throwing you a surprise party. Aaaa I'm sorry. I didn't mean to ruin the surprise! I-If he'll make another one for you, please act surprised! aaa and I'm sorry, I don't have a present for you right now. But I'll get one as soon as possible.' Her face turned completely red. 'I-if you have something you want th-then tell me.' She felt so guilty for what she did, she lifted her head at once; ready to apologize even more.

He just looked at her, smiling. 'Thank you,' he said. He felt so happy and so blessed. He had such great friends who remembered his birthday enough to surprise him. He had his dad and Natalia on his corner. And he had this amazing girl in front of him. What more could he ask for?

The tears started to fall down on their own. He shook his head, 'No.' At first, Anna was worried she might have hurt him with her words, but now his smile was so big she couldn't think that even if she wanted to. She gently touched his cheeks, wiping down the tears and making him laugh. They stared at each other's eyes for god knows how long. Anna didn't realize she fell asleep until she woke up when the train finally stopped. It was early in the morning when she opened her eyes, And even though she spent the night on a train seat; it was the best sleep she had in years. Or maybe it was the best sleep she ever had in her life.

# CHAPTER 45

ANNA SAT ON THE CHAIR INSIDE NATALIA'S CLINIC. IT WAS A dark brown chair made of wooden strings. Natalia had another one like this one, sitting across from Anna. The room had a desk and a double couch as well as white curtains and a grey floor. This room would have seemed to Anna, like any other common office, if it hadn't had something more. On the desk she could see a bunch of Lilies in a red vase with flowers on it. It made her smile. Natalia was a happy person and she had to show it somehow.

Anna recalled, Adrian gave her the number and she called for this appointment just two days ago. It's been almost two weeks since that time on the train when she asked him for her number. She was so nervous when she picked up the phone and called her; that she forgot what they talked about. She just remembered they made the appointment for today, and that's all.

Natalia let her in earlier and went to get them a cup of coffee, and now, she just opened the door and walked in, holding the cups of coffee in her hands. Anna was so nervous she couldn't drink a thing; so she just held the cup and smiled. 'So, why have you decided to come here today?' Natalia asked as she sat down; on the chair across from Anna.

Anna scanned Natalia completely before she answered her question. Natalia was a dark, middle-aged, and a little overweight woman. She looked completely normal, like any other woman her age. But there was something about her Anna just couldn't deny. Her smile made Anna feel more at home than any other place.

'I-I'm..' she started but couldn't finish. The words just refused to come out. She got mad at herself and got up. 'I'm sorry for wasting your time,' she said without looking at her and turned for the door, still holding the cup of coffee in her hand.

Just as she was about to leave, Anna heard her say behind her, 'That's too bad,' she sounded disappointed. 'I was looking forward to meeting you today.' Anna turned back to her, confused. She didn't say anything, so Natalia continued. 'It sounded on the phone like you had so much to say.'

But Anna recalled she was mostly quiet the entire time they spoke over the phone. Then she realized she DID remember the phone call and what exactly happened. She smiled as she realized what Natalia was doing, and she went back to her seat across from her. 'I don't know if you can help me,' she said as she sat down. She sounded so confident, like she was sure that Natalia couldn't. She took a deep breath and let it go before she added, 'But let's find out.'

Anna didn't know what it was exactly about Natalia that made her open up to her like she did. She met this woman today, and she was ready to reveal all of her life's story, like it was as easy as spreading icing on a cake. She told her everything; from Sara to Adam to the Academia. She was even able to say his name in front of her without stopping.

All this time Natalia hasn't said a word. She wrote some things in her notebook, but mostly she concentrated on Anna. She was actually listening to her. Anna hadn't noticed that until she was halfway through her story. 'What?' she stopped and asked when she saw Natalia was smiling. It made her blush and feel selfaware.

'Nothing,' Natalia smiled. 'I'm just so happy you came here today.' She sounded so genuine it made Anna feel more embarrassed than she already was. She wasn't expecting that answer.

'Why?' she asked, but then she changed her mind. 'I-I mean..' tried to say.

'You are stronger than you know, dear.' Natalia sounded so confident when she said that. She sounded like she KNEW Anna really was. 'And it's time you'll know just how much.'

'How?' Anna asked, confused. Natalia sounded so calm and confident in her words; it made her nervous.

'By telling it to yourself,' she said, and it made Anna feel more confused than she was before. Natalia fixed her glasses on her eyes before she spoke. 'You went through all of this and survived. You're a survivor, Anna,' she said. She looked right through her, and Anna felt like she was reading her like an open book. 'Just look at how strong you are. You're still here! Still alive! Someone else in your position would have killed themselves by now! But no! you didn't! That's how strong you are!' she was getting too emotional, saying things she shouldn't. Something about Anna made her this emotional, and she couldn't tell exactly what. But she should be more professional and she calmed herself down.

'But! But!' Anna protested. Her eyes filled up with tears and she turned mad all of a sudden. She refused to look back at Natalia. She refused to believe Natalia's words, even though she knew deep down she was right. For the first time since she walked in, she was crying; and she hated that.

'It's ok,' Natalia said in her old calm voice again. 'You can cry all you want. That doesn't make you any less stronger than you already are.' She got up, took out a tissue box from the inside of one of her desk drawers and gave it to Anna. She was still looking away as she grabbed the box, took out a tissue and wiped her eyes.

'You'll just have to get used to it, dear,' Natalia said as she sat back in her chair. 'Hearing good things about yourself is hard right now, I know. But one day, you'll thank me for saying that. One day you'll thank yourself for saying that.'

Anna was still looking away as she said, 'I don't believe you.'

'I know, dear,' Natalia said. She sounded so confident it made Anna look back at her, shocked. 'But it doesn't matter if you believe me or not right now. My job is to help you believe in yourself, and that's exactly what I'll do.' And she smiled so big it made Anna believe Natalia's words were genuine, even though she didn't believe them herself.

'And how are you going to do that?' she asked, still untrusting.

'Well then,' Natalia said. 'I guess you'll have to tell me more about yourself, first. Then, I'll teach you how,' she smiled and let Anna take away the conversation.

# CHAPTER 46

ANNA STARTED TO COME BY NATALIA'S OFFICE EVERY WEEK. SHE didn't mind the long train ride; Natalia was worth it. And now, she had another reason to go back home. Together they cried, they laughed and they talked about life, Anna's life. They talked about the past, about the present and about the future. She found herself able to tell her things she wasn't able to tell anyone else, including herself. And talking about HIM wasn't excluded.

Anna was still looking away every time she talked about him. The news back then, when the story was on TV for the first time, addressed him in his real name; Max Tribler. But Anna will forever remember him as THE DEAN. She had trouble looking at people's reaction when she told them about him. It was just too much for her.

Natalia listened to her carefully as she told her about the terrible things he had her do back then. Just repeating them out loud was hard enough for her, not to mention telling it while using herself as the main 'heroine' of the story. But part of her treatment was to identify her memories as her own and include herself in the scenarios. It seemed to her sometimes that Natalia set the bar just too high for her to handle..

She jumped up and left the room too many times than she was willing to admit; but Natalia found a way to bring her back every time. She just wasn't ready to give up on her. 'Now, say it like you mean it,' Natalia said and waited for Anna to repeat their mantra.

Anna had to say those words every time before they finished their session. 'I am powerful and strong. There's nothing I can't do,' she said and Natalia smiled.

'Now, how does that make you feel?' she asked.

'Like I can almost believe it,' Anna said and smiled back at her.

'Good,' she said and got off her chair and back to her desk. 'Oh!' she said and stopped; as she recalled something. 'I have been meaning to ask you,' she said and turned back at her. 'Will it be ok if I'd ask you to consider something?'

'What is it?' she asked back. Well, it's true. Old habits do die hard.

'Will you be ok to go and see him at the hospital?' she asked, clearing her intentions.

Anna sank in her thoughts. When they mentioned years back that he was transferred to a mental hospital upstate; she wasn't relieved as others might have thought she would have been. She thought they were too easy on him, and it upset her even more. That was another reason for her efforts to go back to normality and deny everything that was related to that.

But Natalia could see her go under, and she added, 'At least think about it. Adrian also wasn't ready for it when I suggested that to him back then. So I was wondering if the both of you would be ok to do it together?'

Anna raised her eyes off the ground as she spoke in the world's tiniest voice. 'Will you be there?' she asked.

'If you'll have me,' Natalia smiled back an incorrigible smile.

# CHAPTER 47

IT TOOK ABOUT A MONTH OR SO FOR THE BOTH OF THEM TO collect enough courage to go and confront him. THE DEAN was sent; five years ago; to a mental hospital for the criminally insane upstate, just two or three hours drive from their old town. They decided to take Natalia's car, and she came to pick them up from the train station. They sat together in the back seat holding each other's hands. 'Everybody ready?' Natalia turned her head back and looked at them for confirmation. They both nodded their heads up and down, but couldn't say a word.

Anna swore this was the longest drive she ever had in her life. Natalia stopped for a bathroom break every hour, but it only made Anna more anxious. She wanted to be done with that already.

It was already mid-day when they finally got to the hospital. Anna's body was shaking as she stepped off the car and went on the sidewalk. Adrian was ready to run back to the car as he looked at the building. It took everything he had in him to deny that instinct. Natalia held both of their hands and looked at their faces, alternately. 'Ok. Let's go,' she said and they all went inside.

The lady at the reception welcomed them in with a warm smile. She was fully informed of their visit by her manager earlier this morning. He and Natalia went to the same grad school years back; and stayed in touch all this time. She called him last night to clarify this visit. After all, this wasn't a regular inmate they came to visit.

The lady from the front desk led them inside to a large room with a long table, spreading from one side to the next. It had a glass window the same wide, dividing the room into two. It looked the same as they had in jail; only this was used in extreme cases. Normally, the lady at the reception would have taken them to the waiting room, who had tables and chairs for the inmates to sit with their families. But, again, this was not a common inmate.

She sat them at the side of the glass close to them and used a woki-toki machine to communicate with the nurses inside. This was a closed ward and it had maximum security. After she made sure he was on his way, she bedded them goodbye and left.

One of the nurses, a big dark man in blue uniform, walked in front of him, holding the door for him to walk in. HE had trouble crossing by himself and the nurse had to hold the door and help him through at the same time. The years and the medication did him wrong, and he looked like the shadow of the man he used to be. His hair was white, and his face was wrinkled, and he looked twenty years older instead of five. His mouth was drooling, probably due to too many meds. The nurse sat him at the other side of the glass right in front of them.

Adrian smiled an irritated smile. He was furious; someone was definitely kidding him. This wasn't THE DEAN; this was some other lame old man someone scratched off the floors and brought in. He lifted his head, trying to find the hidden cameras he was sure were there.

Anna was shocked when she first saw him. He looked nothing like the man who tortured them all those years ago. This shadow in front of her barely even moved on his own. She couldn't believe her eyes; this was him. She suddenly felt bad for him. He was bound to stay in this place for the rest of his life, too medicated to even know where he was. Suddenly, he looked pitiful in her eyes; like an old man laid on the side of the road.

Natalia looked at the both of them, sitting next to her on both sides. She could hear the wheels inside their heads, processing. 'So,' she said and looked at them, alternately, 'who wants to go first?'

Adrian was the first to respond. He got off his chair so fast, his chair flew behind him onto the entrance door. He was so mad he could break something. 'You, you!' he looked straight at him, through the glass. 'You lame excuse of a man!' he yelled. 'Do you even remember us?' he asked and looked at both Anna and him, alternately. 'Do you even know what you did?!'

While Adrian was letting his rage on, the man across the glass stared at them blankly. He wasn't moving an inch, and it was doubtful if he even knew where he was and what was going on around him. But Adrian didn't care; he wanted to release all the traces of fire left inside of him. To make sure he would leave this place clean.

Anna looked at the old man in front of them, all drooly and disgusting, and she started crying. The tears left on their own as she stood up and looked at him, letting all of her anger out. She moved her hair behind her ear before she opened her mouth to speak. Adrian looked at her rising from her chair, went silent and waited for her to say something. But before she could, the unexpected had happened. The man moved his lips and the tiniest voice was heard. 'My Kitty,' it said.

And even though the man hadn't said nor moved any further, Anna's whole body was on fire. She got closer to the glass, put her hands on it and looked him straight in the eyes. 'My name is Anna,' she said. Then she turned back around and left the room. Anna finished what she came here to do and she had no other reason to stay in this place. Finally, after all of this time, she was done. Really done.

# CHAPTER 48

ANNA WOKE UP IN HER BED, ALONE. SHE LOOKED TO HER SIDES and scanned the room, but she couldn't see it anywhere. She couldn't remember where she left her phone last night. She put his shirt on to cover her naked body, got off the bed, and left the room.

She and her boyfriend moved to this place three years ago, after they both graduated from college. And Anna loved this place. It was a one-hall house, with four bedrooms; which they used as offices. Now, she had to enter every single one of them in order to find her phone. And where is her boyfriend anyway? It's Saturday today. He should be still sleeping like a log right now.

Anna walked to her boyfriend's office; a small room with a desk and a laptop on top, a spinning chair, and some pens and markers on the desk. And the whole room was covered with pages. She knew she had no point in telling him to clean it up; her office looked even worse. Anyway, once he'll finish his next issue and post it on his website, this room will go back to its normal state.

She scanned the room completely before she finally found it lying between all the pages scattered on the table. She was about to leave the room when something caught the corner of her eye. The characters looked different than the ones he usually draws. She looked between the pages, found the first one and started to read.

It was a comic book story about a female scientist who wanted to create the ultimate medicine and help sick children in the hospital she worked in. So, she created this new formula, but something went wrong in the experiment and it blew up. The female scientist didn't die from the explosion; on the contrary, it gave her super powers. Now, she could fly, lift heavy things and shoot lasers out of her eyes. Something like a modern superhero story.

The story continues as the scientist's sidekick, a nerdy male doctor, who helped her with the experiment, is now left alone. He creates a replica of her formula, only he makes too much of it. He is about to drink it when she flys in and breaks the test tube before he's able to. She convinces him to choose life and she tells him she loves him. He asks her to date him and she agrees. Sometime later, he goes down on one knee, holding a box with a diamond ring and asks, 'Will you marry me?'

Anna grabbed all the pages on the desk. She picked them up and tossed them on the desk, over and over again, but she couldn't find the rest. 'No way! You can't leave it like that! I have to know what happens next!' she yelled and got up. It was only now that she found what she was looking for. Adrian was in his underwear, on one knee, holding a box with a diamond ring and asked, 'Will you marry me?'

She got used to it by now; the way this man kept asking her questions she had no answers to. And usually she wouldn't react to him or try to answer his questions; only this time she had a good answer.

It's funny, actually, how things turn up; and how in just a couple of years a person could change so drastically. Because, if someone had asked five years ago's Anna if she ever thought about getting married, she'd probably say she won't ever EVER do that. And if they'd ask three years ago's Anna, she'd probably say she won't; but if she had, Adrian would be a good option for that. Last year's Anna would have said she's not waiting for him to ask her, but she wouldn't mind if he did. And this moment's Anna was over the moon.

She was so happy she had trouble speaking. Her legs gave up and she fell on her knees, right in front of him. The tears started falling on their own. He put his hand on her cheek, wiping them away. 'Are you ok?' he asked. She nodded and sniffed.

Anna put her arms around Adrian's neck and pulled him close. Their foreheads touched as she closed her eyes, took a deep breath and let it go. 'Thank you,' she said, her eyes still closed.

He smiled. 'What for?' he asked. He closed his eyes and let her take him with her.

'Thank you for not giving up on me,' she said, between deep breaths. 'Thank you for always being on my side,' another deep breath, 'and thank you for asking the right question, this time.'

He opened his eyes and moved his head back. 'I'll take that as a yes?' he asked, all smiling. She opened her eyes and nodded her head slowly, up and down. He leaned in and kissed her lips firmly, holding her face in one hand and her back with the other.

They slowed down the kiss and clenched their foreheads together again. 'Thank you for doing the same,' he said smiling. His whole body was shaking from her touch. Now, it was his turn to shed some tears.

Anna closed her eyes and smiled. 'Anytime,' she said.

# CHAPTER 49

THE OPENING TITLES FOR THE MOST VIEWED MORNING TALK show, 'Sunny side up,' went on; as the host, Sunny Michaels, sat in front of the camera and prepared for today's live show. She looked straight to the camera, took a deep breath and waited for her turn to speak. She was especially excited today; one of her female idols was coming to the show for an interview. Once the music ended and the producer marked her cue, she put her game face on.

'Hello everyone!' she said in her usual hype voice, 'and thank you for joining us at the Sunny side up, morning talk show, the best talk show in this hemisphere. Today we have some surprises for you, but I won't spoil them. You'll have to stay with us to find out,' she winked at the camera. 'But to get things started, I'm more than happy to welcome in our first guest,' she took a deep breath and let go.

'She's the owner and founder of the A-Corporation, that provides many technological solutions worldwide, and she's responsible for so many technological discoveries and inventions. She's a wonderful mom for three incredible children and she's married to an anonymous comic artist, some of you may know..' She gave the audience another wink and some of them started to laugh. 'She's here to promote her first book. Let's give a big round of applause for Anna Martinez!' Sunny got off of her chair and applauded with the rest of the audience as Anna walked into the studio.

Anna thought she'd get used to it by now. Over the past years she had multiple interviews to many TV and radio programs, but every single time she had that feeling in her stomach. That feeling she had back when she was fourteen, that feeling that will probably never go away. The one she keeps waking up to, every now and then; the useless one. She could feel that especially in these kinds of times, when she was the center of people's attention. Like they could look inside her and see that she was full of nothing. She had no choice but to confront this feeling every single time and push through, including right now.

She shook Sunny's hand and sat on one of the two couches next to her; on the one closest to her, and waved to the audience. After the applause settled down, Sunny turned to her guest. She was more than excited to do this interview, and she thanked the good lord in her heart she had the chance to do it. 'Thank you for joining us today, Anna,' she smiled.

'Thank you for having me,' Anna smiled back. These kinds of things still stressed her out, and she found herself still looking for the exits. She smiled deep down, took a deep breath and reminded herself she had to face this head on. 'I can do this!' she calmed herself down. 'I am powerful and strong. There's nothing I can't do.'

'So please tell us about your new book.' Sunny picked up the book off a small table next to her, right between her and Anna, and showed it to the camera. 'I understand you wrote it about your own personal experience,' she looked at Anna like she just asked her a question and she was waiting for an answer.

'Yes,' Anna replied. 'It is. I wrote about my own experiences from when I was a kid.'

Sunny looked at her idol amazed. 'That's incredible,' she said and then reminded they weren't alone, just the two of them. 'For those of you who don't know,' she turned to the audience and the camera. 'Anna recently shared on her social media she was sexually harassed and abused as a child.' Some of the people in the audience gasped and some yelled and cursed.

Anna nodded slowly. She should have been used to those words by now; it's been so long ago, but they still hurt her every single time. She took a deep breath and let go before she started talking. 'You can find the whole story in the book,' she smiled at the audience, and they, in return, applauded.

'And everyone here at the studio gets a free copy,' Sunny said in her hype voice and smiled. That made them cheer and applauded even louder.

'So, tell me,' Sunny said as the applause settled down. 'What made you want to share your story now? what changed?' Anna looked at her without saying a word, so she added, 'I'm only saying that since you never mentioned that part of your life before.' She turned to the audience for agreement. 'I don't remember ever seeing or reading anything about that that's related to you.'

Anna sat up straight in her seat before she spoke. She looked so serious all of a sudden. 'I think I can explain that better now,' she said and moved her hair behind her ear. 'You see, all my life I have been running away from myself, trying to deny it, like it never even happened to me. It took me a long time to realize that I needed to face and deal with it. I never even realized I needed help,' she had a confident smile on her face when she talked; one could see she was getting more and more confident as she went on.

'So this book is like another form of therapy to you?' Sunny asked. She and the audience listen to her with care. Anna has gotten so serious so fast they didn't expect it. Her words made them want to listen since she had so much strength in her tone.

'I guess you can say that, in a way.. I had to go through a lot before I turned for help. But luckily for me, help knocked on my door before I had the chance to,' she laughed.

'What do you mean?' Sunny took the bait.

'I guess you'll have to read my book if you want to know.' Anna said and smiled like she had a big secret she wasn't telling, making the audience burst with laughter. Sunny smiled and fought the urge to join them. Her guest was one clever cookie, and she never saw it coming. While the producers tried to calm the audience down, the director of the show talked to her inside her ear and distracted her from these events.

Sunny touched her earpiece and nodded her head up and down to show the director she understood what he said. She waited for the audience to settle down before she said, 'We have a surprise for you.' All smiling like she had a secret. She was wearing a mischief look on her face, as she said that, and Anna's heart started pounding, nervous.

'He's one of the most known comic artists nowadays.' Sunny used the same hype voice she used to welcome Anna to the show, to welcome her second guest. 'Every issue he puts out is sold out within seconds. The movie adaptation to one of his stories turned into one of the most earning blockbusters last year.' Then she looked at Anna with mischief, 'and he is married to someone you may know..' Anna started laughing, super surprised. Sunny stood up and added, 'Please welcome in Adrian Martinez,' and the crowd went nuts.

Adrian walked in, waving at the crowd, but stopped and started laughing when he saw his wife's reaction; she was looking back at him and laughing. He winked at her and said, taunting, 'Did you miss me?' the whole crowd applauded so loud it took the producers a while to settle them down. Adrian sat at the chair next to Anna after he shook Sunny's hand.

Anna punched her husband's shoulder and he started laughing again. Sunny looked at them, amused. 'So I guess this means we succeeded at surprising you.' she said.

'This guy!' Anna jumped up in her seat and pointed at Adrian. 'Saw me getting ready for this show just two hours ago and didn't say a thing! Even when I told him I was coming here today!' She seemed to be more loose and herself once he was on her side. 'I was like I'm going to the Sunny Michaels' show today, and he was like; oh, ok. Have fun!' She copied their conversation from earlier this morning and then gave her husband a fake angry look. She was being funny and made everyone else start laughing.

Sunny was laughing as well and had trouble keeping talking. She had to look away, take a few deep breaths in order to keep going. 'Well, I'm glad our plan to surprise you today worked.' she fought the urge to burst into laughter again. 'But we have another reason why we brought your husband here today,' she cleared her throat to sound more serious. 'Not to talk about his well-known, many achievements,' she winked at him and got some positive comments from the crowd for that. 'But today we're here to talk about your new book.' She turned back to Anna. 'I was told your husband's story is also in there.'

Anna and Adrian switched looks and smiled back at each other a comforting smile before she answered the question. 'Yes. He and I met through that experience.' It was clear it was still painful for her to talk about it.

'But we didn't recognize each other after that,' Adrian completed the sentence for her.

'So you two met there but didn't remember each other when you met again?' Sunny asked. It was her obligation as the host to make the information as understandable as possible for the people watching her; even though she couldn't reveal all the information, her guests didn't want her to.

'Exactly,' Adrian conformed.

'So, how did you find out you both had the same experience?' Sunny kept going.

Anna smiled, 'That's in the book.' It made everyone, including Sunny and her husband, start laughing. Sunny nodded at her idol with respect.

Sunny stopped to think as the audience was calming down; and once they did, she asked, 'So, how did that make you, Adrian,' she turned to him, 'feel when your wife decided to write your story, so exposed like that? After all, it's your past as well.'

'True,' he said and smiled, recalling at that time when he and Anna had that conversation. 'At first I was like, hell no!' and the crowd started laughing. Sunny looked at him with a scolding face. Adrian grinned and added shyly, 'Forgive me for my french.'

'Ok,' She gave him a testing look and continued, 'and then what?'

'It sounded too revealing for me, and you know me, I'm an open book.' He gave Sunny another look and turned back to his wife. 'But then she told me why she wanted to write our story,' he acted mysteriously for a moment and then smiled.

That made Sunny curious, and she decided to bite again. 'Why?' she asked.

Adrian looked at Anna like he was asking her permission to quote her. She nodded softly and he continued. She said, 'You taught me it was ok to open up and let go of the pain. Now, we have the privilege to teach others to do the same,' when they heard his words, the crowd made sounds of admiration and appreciation.

Sunny looked at her idol proudly. She knew she had a good reason to look up to this woman. 'That's what we wanted to do with this book,' Anna followed her husband's words.'To show everyone, boys and girls, who went through something like that. Well, our story is a bit extreme...' she gave the audience a secret-like look. 'But to those who experienced the worst, we wanted to show them that they could find a way to come back from that and be happy. By sharing, by KNOWING they're not alone. By showing them how to confront their inner demons and that they too deserve to be happy.'

The audience couldn't agree more, and they clapped and cheered for her once again. This time, the producers joined as well, and it made Anna turn shy. While the cheerings slowly calmed down, Sunny listened to her director, talking in her ear, one more time.

'I'd like to share with our viewers and audience today that,' she said when the studio was finally quiet again. 'You two have a non-profit organization that helps kids and young-adult who were sexually abused, called...'

'Running together,' Adrian added while smiling. It always made him laugh a little since they chose that name. It had a nice pun in it.

'Yes,' Sunny said and turned to the viewers watching her at home. 'They provide psychological, personal and legal aid for kids and young adults who were abused and sexually abused. Their number is now on the screen. You can call them about yourselves and if you see someone you feel needs help in these aspects, they can help.'

'Right,' Anna said and their both nodded in agreement.

'Thank you, both of you,' Sunny said and looked at her guests. 'For coming to the show today,' she put her hands together in a Namaste gesture, and nodded her head up and down towards them. They nodded back. 'And you,' she turned to her viewers, lowering her hands and changing her tune, back to her usual hype self. 'Stay tuned for more of Sunny side up, when we come back after this,' the commercial titles went on and the show went off the air.

Printed in Great Britain
by Amazon

69782502R00123